RELUCTANT PROMISE

Ann Redmayne

CHIVERS
THORNDIKE

This Large Print edition is published by BBC Audiobooks Ltd, Bath, England and by Thorndike Press®, Waterville, Maine, USA.

Published in 2004 in the U.K. by arrangement with the author.

Published in 2004 in the U.S. by arrangement with Juliet Burton Literary Agency.

U.K. Hardcover ISBN 0–7540–7704–7 (Chivers Large Print)
U.K. Softcover ISBN 0–7540–7705–5 (Camden Large Print)
U.S. Softcover ISBN 0–7862–5950–7 (Nightingale)

The text of this Large Print edition is unabridged.
Other aspects of the book may vary from the original edition.

Set in 16 pt. New Times Roman.

Printed in Great Britain on acid-free paper.

British Library Cataloguing in Publication Data available

Library of Congress Cataloging-in-Publication Data

Redmayne, Ann.
  Reluctant promise / by Ann Redmayne.
    p.   cm.
  ISBN 0–7862–5950–7 (lg. print : sc : alk. paper)
  1. Triangles (Interpersonal relations)—Fiction.
  2. England—Fiction. 3. Large type books. I. Title.
PR6118.E45R43 2003
823'.92—dc22   2003061636

CHAPTER ONE

Primrose Edmunds and Barney Tabley could not have been said to have grown up together, for they were of different social classes. But being neighbours, even the strictures of the years leading up to 1915 could not keep them totally apart.

Primrose, or Rose as she preferred to be called, was the only daughter of a well-regarded, prosperous, Worcestershire farmer, Edward Edmunds. Although most men with such a large acreage would not have dirtied their hands, even in peacetime Barney had worked the same hours as his labourers, with the same degree of hard, physical work. By comparison, Barney's widowed mother enjoyed cultivating the aura of gentility she felt went with being Lady of the Manor.

The corn was standing in stocks in one of Edward Edmunds' fields when Barney seemed to chance upon Rose. She had come looking for an empty stone jar for farm-brewed cider left by the farmhands, whilst he was supposedly going to join the agent who ran the family estate.

'Rose, hello, fancy meeting you!' Barney called through a thin part of the hawthorn hedge dividing the two properties. 'Your magnetic personality is drawing me to you yet again.'

Although this was Barney's latest exaggerated greeting and would in a few weeks become a little tedious, Rose had to laugh as with loud protestations and wild waving of his arms, he pretended to be dragged through the hedge by an invisible force.

'I'll need first aid after this,' he warned, crashing through the final prickly branches.

'Then go to Mrs Peters,' Rose replied pertly, arms akimbo, hands nearly spanning the small waist of her serviceable navy skirt. 'She'll be happy to pour iodine on your wounds.'

'She's a torturer masquerading as a housekeeper. Rose, have pity on me!' he begged with such a comic look of agony that she went to give him a playful push.

'Got you!' Barney yelled victoriously, grabbing her arms.

Although, as they both left childhood behind, Barney had held her hand or snatched a kiss, lately Rose had become aware of a new forcefulness about him. His kisses had become more demanding as he used his superior strength to stop her escaping. Sometimes he frightened her a little, although at eighteen she considered herself to be adult, able to cope with anything.

'Barney, stop it!' she protested as they tumbled backward into a corn stook, which collapsed, spiking them with sharp stalks.

2

Then looking up at him and seeing his eyes gleaming with a strange excitement, a totally foreign emotion engulfed her. Fear jerked her into frenzied action, clenched fists pummelling him.

'Stop it! Let me up!' she half ordered, half pleaded.

As he bent to kiss her, she jerked her head from side to side. That this was no playful, romantic dalliance gave strength to her evasive actions, her lips sealed against his.

'Come on, Rose, what's the matter with you? It's only a game. Or are you trying to live up to your name of being a prim rose?' he taunted.

Then a darkening shadow fell across them and Barney was cursing with pain as his arm was expertly twisted up behind him. As soon as she felt his body weight lift from her, Rose scrambled up, her back to the two men, as she hastily adjusted the modest neck of her white cotton blouse, then raked away long strands of sun-bleached hair from her face.

Barney tried to jab his free elbow into his captor's body.

'If it's a fight you want, then I'm happy to oblige,' was the almost lazy challenge.

Rose caught her breath as she recognised Hugo Smith's deep voice. He often came to the farm for milk, butter and eggs, and for some reason she could not understand, she immediately felt mortified that it was he who

3

had rescued her, not some local man.

'Please don't fight,' she begged, turning to face him. 'It's nothing.'

Releasing Barney with a jerk of contempt, Hugo regarded her reflectively.

'It didn't look like nothing to me, or were your protestations all part of the game? If so, Miss Edmunds, I hope you are aware of all the rules, for you were indulging in a dangerous amusement.'

'Barney startled me. There's no harm done.'

'Maybe not this time.'

'What's it to you?' Barney demanded belligerently. 'This is private land.'

'If I'm trespassing, then so are you,' Hugo reminded evenly. 'But as I'm going up to the Edmunds' farm, I think I have a little more right to be on their land than you.'

Barney did not get a chance to reply, for with cool politeness, Hugo was offering to accompany Rose back home, just as soon as he retrieved the pint milk-can which he had thrown down on seeing the struggle.

To a casual observer, Rose's hazel eyes might have been downcast demurely, but in reality, she could not bring herself to look directly at either her tormentor or rescuer, the one for anger, the other for shame. Leaving Barney to crash his way back through the hedge, Rose and Hugo walked in silence until he went to open the five-barred gate.

Glancing up to thank him, Rose rushed out,

'It isn't what you think. Barney's never been like that before.'

'In that case, take it as a warning. There's a whole world of difference between a kiss freely given and one taken by force, especially by an inexperienced boy.'

'He's not a boy, he's twenty,' she corrected quickly, wanting to dispel the idea Hugo might have of Barney and her being just children.

Shutting the gate behind them, Hugo tried to lighten the atmosphere, asking about the haymaking and relieved, Rose answered with almost childlike eagerness. Thinking about the family farm meant she could push Barney to the back of her mind.

Practised at concealing his feelings, his true self, Hugo continued easily.

'Having seen you in the hayfields and driving the carthorses I realise you have to help since your young labourers are in the army, but you seem to enjoy it.'

'I know it's not the done thing, but yes, I do enjoy helping with the outdoor work and with the animals. My father says I can coax milk out of the most difficult cow.'

He nodded as though he understood, and seeing this made Rose question boldly, 'Why do you shut yourself up in that cottage by the lake to write? I thought authors starved in cold city garrets.'

'Luckily I've money enough not to starve and as I like the country, I force myself to put up with a reasonably comfortable cottage, rather than a garret. I hope I haven't disappointed you.'

He smiled. Then seeing they were nearing the farm, he added softly, 'Don't worry, I won't say anything, but, Miss Primrose Edmunds, remember that although your namesake flower seems hardy, flowering as it does in sometimes harsh weather, it can be easily damaged by a careless hand.'

Apart from the few words necessary as Rose filled his milk-can in the dairy, Hugo left with his usual courteous farewell. Watching as he strode easily across the cobbled farmyard, she frowned, and not for the first time, she wondered about him. What did Hugo write about? Did all writers shut themselves away in near isolation? Rose reddened. What on earth was she doing thinking about a man who must be thirty if he was a day? Then with a single-mindedness that some called stubbornness, she busied herself with work about the farm and house.

'It's no good, I can't keep my prices down any longer,' Edward worried aloud over the supper table that evening. 'I know food prices are already way above pre-war, but my costs have soared, too.'

As usual, his wife, Flora, was wrapped in daydreams and not for the first time, Rose glared impatiently at her. Why couldn't her mother be more of a support to her father?

Rose used to be fascinated by Flora's eccentricity, but since the outbreak of war, with all the extra strain it brought in running the farm, she wished her mother was less interested in painting flower pictures which never sold and making up herbal concoctions. It was this absorption with plants that had brought about Primrose being named after the flowers blooming at the time of her birth.

Still grim-faced, Edward continued.

'When Old Joe was doing the milk round this morning he heard that two more village lads have been killed. One of them was Bob Fielding. It seems like only yesterday that he gave me a hand repairing the cowshed roof.'

'Oh, no, not Bob!' Rose exclaimed, eyes filling with tears.

Always deeply upset by news of yet another death or wounding, that Bob was younger than her hit harder.

'That's the second son the Fieldings have lost,' she added. 'I must go over and see them, take them a pie, perhaps a cake.'

'That sort of thing isn't for a young girl. Your mother should do it.'

As they both glanced without much hope at Flora, she smiled vaguely. 'Rose is so much better at that sort of thing than I am. But I'll make up a bottle of my tonic for them. In fact I'll go and do it now.'

With far more purpose than she used for domestic chores, Flora left the table, hurrying towards the little outhouse she called her distilling room.

'Sorry, Rose.'

Although Edward's tone was apologetic, his face was set as he left the table. Not for the first time he wondered what on earth had possessed him to marry Flora instead of a down-to-earth farmer's daughter. But he had been young, taken with her feyness and when she had favoured him with her charm, he had been completely bowled over.

Rose slept fitfully that night, dreams vividly reflecting her chaotic thoughts. Barney . . . Bob . . . carefree years banished by war and the totally unexpected happenings of the day.

The next morning, she did not linger at the Fieldings' cottage for she felt very out of place amongst the village women already gathered there. Also, from past experience she knew only too well there would be nudges and knowing looks because she had come, not her mother. Flora had never made the slightest attempt to be part of village life.

Just as she was leaving the cottage, Rose met Mrs Tabley, who greeted her with the tight-lipped smile she considered to be ladylike.

'Your mother not here, child?'

Suddenly tired of making excuses for her mother's absences, Rose did not bother to reply, but just stood to one side to give Mrs Tabley's ample figure more room on the narrow garden path.

'Go and wait with Barney,' she was ordered. 'We passed an undesirable on the way here and I would not wish any daughter of mine to be roaming about by herself.'

At this mention of Barney, Rose's body stiffened. She was far from ready to meet him, not until she had sorted out her feelings about him, how to treat him now that he had upset the happy, carefree balance of their long friendship. Quickly darting around the back of the cottage, she hurried through the vegetable garden and, hitching up her skirt, began scrambling over the low stone wall into a field. But to her consternation Barney suddenly appeared, and although he did not look directly at her, he offered a helping hand.

Pointedly ignoring it, she lowered herself on to the tussocky grass and would have walked away resolutely had he not rushed out an obviously abject apology.

'Rose, I'm truly sorry about yesterday. I didn't mean to frighten you. That's the last thing I would do. I don't know what came over me.'

'It's all right,' she interrupted awkwardly, not looking at him for fear she would glimpse something of the hot-blooded Barney of the cornfield.

To his obvious relief, she stayed, but evaded his pleading eyes, for happy memories of their growing-up years were beginning to soften the edges of her jagged emotions. Perhaps it all had been just fooling about which had got out of hand.

'No, it isn't all right!' he corrected harshly. 'I shouldn't have been so . . .'

Then unable to find the right words for his so recently recognised, but totally unexpected feelings for her, he finished lamely, 'I got carried away.'

Looking directly at him for the first time, and seeing his penitent expression, she was nevertheless startled to hear herself saying lightly, 'You nearly were, by Mr Smith!'

As Barney thrust his hands into his trouser pockets and shuffled an awkward foot through the buttercup-bright grass, Rose suppressed a bubble of laughter. When he was a lad he had often looked like that when Mrs Tabley had lectured him about some small misdemeanour. But swiftly composing herself, she nodded in agreement when he answered.

'If it had to be anyone, I'm glad it was him and not a village lad, for by now your father would be after me with a shotgun.'

Rose had an almost overpowering urge to try to retrieve their previous relationship, unsullied as it had been by adult emotions.

'So what sort of pest do you see yourself as that needs shooting? A fox? A pigeon?'

Offering his hand, Barney looked down at her with a seriousness she had seldom seen before.

'Rose, I don't think you realise we're not children any more. I know we've fooled around before, throwing hay, then collapsing out of breath. Yesterday, though, was different. You might not sense or even want any change in our relationship, but over the last few months I've become very aware that you are a very attractive girl. Perhaps it's something to do with the war, the uncertainties.'

'Barney, I'm flattered, but please don't spoil things,' she rushed out. 'I realise now that we can't fool around like we used to do, but I still want us to be friends, just friends,' she repeated.

'Just friends,' he repeated softly, placing a tender kiss on her hand.

As Rose turned to hurry away across the field, she glimpsed someone in the nearby hazel coppice and groaned. It wouldn't take long for the much-embroidered news to reach her father that Barney had been seen kissing her, even though it had only been her hand!

Over the next few days, Rose felt saddened that the carefree, casual relationship she had shared with Barney had gone for ever. Wherever she went, he seemed to be there, too, looking at her with dark, contemplative eyes. But then, like everyone else in the neighbourhood, she was caught up in the excitement of two local lads returning from France. Both had been seriously wounded, Jim

Shepherd suffering a head wound which had left his senses impaired whilst Andrew Jones had lost a leg.

Rose was busy in the dairy when Barney came with the governess cart to pick up some hens to replace those thieved by a fox, and through the window she saw him talking to her father. There was something about their manner which made her stop and move closer to the open door.

'I didn't know what to say when I came across Andrew just now in the village,' Barney was saying. 'Seeing him hopping about on crutches took the wind right out of my sails. But what really shocked me was that he was whistling as though he hadn't a care in the world!'

'Well, in a way he hasn't, not now. Neither he nor Jim will have to go back to the hell of that war.'

'My mother . . .' Barney began, then turned away to soothe the restless old pony, the only carriage horse left to them by the army.

'She doesn't want you to go,' Edward finished. 'It's understandable, you being her only child and needed to keep the estate going.'

'But I'm not a child!'

Barney's vehement reply and what it implied made Rose gasp with shock. Even when most of the local able-bodied young men had enlisted, she had never considered he might do so. He was part of her childhood, when the world had seemed a safe, unchanging place.

'So you're thinking of going then?' Edward asked.

'Seeing Andrew has made me do more than just think. No doubt Mother will have one of her turns as she always does when thwarted, so It will be a week or two before I enlist. As for the estate, Sims can postpone his retirement. He's always saying he has more go in him at seventy than someone half his age.'

'Wouldn't it be kinder to your mother to go now rather than draw it out?'

'I suppose it might be, but I've a few things to sort out first.'

Putting his hand on Barney's shoulder, Edward reassured, 'I'll do all I can to help at the manor, and I know Rose will call to see your mother. She might be glad of young company when you've gone.'

Slumped against the hard, stone working surfaces of the dairy, Rose bowed her head, hands covering her face as though fending off unnamed future horrors.

* * *

There were a few wealthy women in Worcester who swore that Flora's cowslip cream kept their skin youthful and when they ordered by letter, it was Rose who had the job of taking

13

the parcel to the village post office.

After overhearing her father and Edward, combined with seeing Andrew and Jim at church on Sunday, beauty cream seemed insultingly frivolous. What did a few wrinkles matter when men were dying or left horribly maimed? So it was with ill grace that she set off with the latest parcel.

Opening the post office door, the usual ting of the bell was lost in several loud voices, for unlike most men, Saul, the postmaster, loved a gossip.

Glimpsing Rose, he exclaimed gleefully, 'Now here's someone who might know something, for he goes to the Edmunds' farm for his milk. That there man who's renting the cottage by the lake, Rose, what do you know about him? He never gets any letters, only strange telegrams I can't make head nor tail of.'

'He's a writer,' Rose replied shortly, as the women made way for her to reach the small counter.

'What, books and the like?' Saul asked.

Then seeing the address on Rose's parcel, he pounced on another topic.

'You send a lot of parcels to Worcester. There must be someone there who likes your butter.'

Despite Saul's most vigorous probings Rose had never divulged the contents of the parcels, nor contradicted when he hit upon the idea

14

that they contained butter.

'That man,' another woman reminded Rose, 'you must have learned something about him. Doesn't he talk to your father, or Barney Tabley?'

'I wouldn't know. We never talk about Mr Smith.'

'I expect you and Barney are too busy making sheep's eyes at each other,' someone said. 'Barney'd make a good catch for you.'

'There's nothing like that,' Rose denied hotly. 'Barney and I have been friends all our lives.'

Embarrassment making her clumsy, she dropped the coins she was getting out of her purse and as she bent to retrieve them, one of the younger women stooped to help her.

'They don't mean no harm,' she whispered. 'A bit of teasing helps them forget the misery of this war. They know full well hoity-toity Mrs Tabley wouldn't let her son marry beneath him.'

Her transaction completed, Rose hurried out, smarting from those two words 'beneath him'. In no hurry to reach home Rose walked up the lane away from the village. She was well aware people did not marry out of their class, although her mother frequently hinted she had done so. But having grown up with Barney and no barrier having been placed to stop their friendship, it had come as a shock to hear it said she was beneath him. Of course she had

15

never been asked to the manor for social occasions, had never been invited to Barney's childhood birthday parties, nor him to hers.

'Good day, Miss Edmunds. May I walk with you or would you prefer to be left alone with your thoughts?'

Hugo Smith was coming towards her down the track from his cottage. She reddened as she recalled the talk in the post office. Then eager to banish all she had heard there, she nodded her acceptance. For a minute or so they continued along the lane in a silence Rose found companionable, reassuring, but then she supposed that he being a stranger would not be interested in local gossip. But next instant she was proved wrong.

'You looked downcast when I saw you. Was it because of the two lads who have just come back? You must have known them all your life and that must make their dreadful plight more personal, painful.'

'Barney has heard Andrew whistling. I don't understand how he can be so cheerful with only one leg. I would be devastated.'

'You haven't seen the carnage at the front.'

There was something in Hugo's voice, a bitter hardness, which made Rose slant a quick glance at his profile.

'You've been there, haven't you?' she asked softly.

He nodded, then as he turned towards her, they both stopped. When she saw the pain in his eyes, her hand moved as though to comfort him but something in his rigid manner warned that such a gesture would not be welcome.

'I would ask you, Miss Edmunds, not to divulge this. There are things in this world which should not be belittled by wagging village tongues.'

'I'll have you know I'm no village gossip!'

'I never meant to imply such a thing. Recently I've been so much by myself that even innocent idle chatter jars.'

'Do you always need solitude for your writing?'

'To think clearly, yes.'

'Are your books very clever?' she asked with eager innocence.

'They're not clever as you mean it. What I write is . . . er . . . necessary.'

Then the sharp persistent ringing of a bicycle bell had them both looking up the lane to where Barney was pedalling furiously towards them.

'Do you wish me to stay?' Hugo asked. 'Though I guess Barney's heightened colour today is caused only by his exertions.'

Flustered by this reminder of the previous time Hugo had seen them together, Rose did not know how to answer. If she said she did not want him to stay, might this imply she wanted to be alone with Barney? On the other hand, if she did ask him to remain, would he take it to mean that she did not want to be alone with Barney? Seeing her obvious confusion, Hugo's smile encompassed both Rose and Barney, whose violent application of the brakes threatened to catapult him over the handlebars.

'Careful!' Rose warned, then laughed as Barney pretended to be on a bucking horse, but her laughter was cut short by his abrupt change from joking to a sullen frown.

'What were you two talking about? Me?'

'Don't be so ridiculous! We were just passing the time of day.'

She turned to Hugo for confirmation but he had gone, striding back towards his cottage.

'In that case, why has he gone off like that?'

'He doesn't like chatting much.'

'Told you that, did he? He seemed to be enjoying chatting to you!'

'Barney, I do believe you're jealous!'

She had meant this as a tease but to her surprise he dropped his bike and, taking both of her hands, looked at her intensely which made her catch her breath. Surely he wasn't going to try anything akin to what had happened in the cornfield? No, she reasoned. The lane was far too public.

'I'm jealous every time another man looks at you. The village lads are bad enough, but he's different. He's not one of us. There's something about him, something a girl might find very attractive.'

'Meaning me?' Rose asked quietly.

18

Looking down at her hands and rubbing his thumbs over her sun-browned skin, he nodded slowly. Head on one side to look up into his face, Rose intended saying she was not attracted to Hugo, but Barney suddenly straightened as though with resolve.

'Rose, I'm going to enlist.'

He paused, wanting her to exclaim in dismay, but she was silent. Her eyes though were full of compassion, shadowed by worry.

'I would go with a lighter step if I knew you wouldn't get entangled with anyone,' Barney was rushing on.

'Wedding bells don't interest me. I'm happy as I am,' Rose answered.

'Not now perhaps, but next year, next month even.'

'Barney, with all the men of my age in the army, there's no-one left.'

'There are heroes like Jim and Andrew. Pity can do strange things.'

'Not to me!' she denied almost fiercely.

This seemed to break the intense atmosphere which had built up and they both smiled, but as their eyes met, Barney drew her closer to him. Knowing he was going to kiss her, she tensed, heart hammering. But when his lips met hers, they were so gentle that she responded out of relief.

'Rose,' he whispered against her cheek. 'I...'

But he got no further as a hay cart came

rumbling down the lane. He dropped her hands and, picking up his bike, sped away whistling happily. As she watched him go, a shiver of disquiet had her hunching her shoulders.

CHAPTER TWO

When Mrs Tabley took to her bed with a turn it did not warrant more than just a mention in the village. Although Rose and her father did not mention it to each other, they both guessed the reason for this latest indisposition was that Barney had told his mother of his intention to enlist.

Going into the village general store on the Monday morning, Rose knew instantly that something serious had happened, for instead of being busy at their washtubs, disapproving women were standing in groups, their voices from a distance sounding like a swarm of angry bees.

'What's happened?' Rose asked anxiously, edging her way into the group.

'It's downright wicked, that's what I say,' Bertha Bridges exclaimed. 'If I had my way, I'd give 'em both a good thrashing.'

'Why it's those two hussies from Middle Hayford,' another snapped.

Amidst murmurs of agreement, Rose

demanded, 'What two girls? What's happened?'

'Them two what's given their all for King and country have been dumped, that's what!' was the grim reply.

Seeing Rose's puzzled frown, Bertha was only too eager to oblige.

'It's Jim and Andy. Those two girls they were courting have turned against them. They've gone and taken up with two other men.'

'So how are Jim and Andy taking it?' Rose asked.

'How do you think? Andy got roaring drunk at The Drovers last night and that poor lad, Jim, well, his mother isn't sure he really does understand what's happened, him being addled in the head. Just as well really, for of the two lads, he was the one with the hottest temper.'

With a vague nod, Rose hurried away, so upset that she forgot her shopping. How could those two girls be so cruel? Once out of sight of the village, she sank down on a grassy bank as she buried her head in her hands. Those poor lads. Wasn't it enough that they had suffered such terrible injuries?

'So you've heard then?'

Lifting her head slowly, Rose looked up blankly at Hugo.

'Bad news reaches even me in my country garret,' he said softly. 'I was out walking very

21

early and met a poacher. To distract me from the two rabbits bulging in his pockets, he told me what had happened.'

As he sat down beside her, unhappy though she was, she noticed that he did not take advantage of the situation by sitting too close as village lads or Barney would have done.

'Would it help to talk?' he offered. 'As I really didn't know the two lads, my emotions won't match yours, but that isn't to say I don't feel for them.'

Then the dam holding back her emotions broke. Although Hugo had to listen intently to keep hold of the threads of her outpourings, he forced himself to resist the nearly overpowering urge to put his arm around Rose, to draw her close, to comfort her.

'Sorry, you must think I'm silly,' she gulped out eventually, 'but suddenly life's so horrible. Perhaps it always has been and I've been too unworldly to realise it.'

'No, I don't think you're silly,' Hugo replied. 'But even if there hadn't been this terrible war, there does come a time in most people's lives when they suddenly realise life isn't all blue summer skies.'

'I know that!' she retorted shortly. 'Failed harvests, accidents, illnesses, children dying too young, but life's always been like that and we have to accept it. This war though, it's so all-consuming and there doesn't seem to be an end. With bad harvests there's always the hope next year's will be better. But will next year be better?'

'I just don't know.'

'But what can I do?' she said in frustration.

'Help keep the farm going, support people.'

'You mean people like Jim and Andy?' she seized upon eagerly.

'Not only them, but the people involved with them. It isn't always the obvious like wounded men and bereaved families who suffer. There are so many ways of helping, some not always very apparent. Supporting others so they can play an active part is really doing something.'

'I don't see how.'

'You will, when the time comes,' he said quietly, then, nodding towards her empty basket, he asked, 'If you're going to the shops, perhaps I might walk with you. Although it means fending off yet another interrogation from Saul, I do need postage stamps.'

Getting to his feet, Hugo held out his hand to help her rise, but when they were standing facing each other, he continued to hold her hand gently. Rose realised that never before had she felt so comforted, reassured, but seeing her glance down at their joined hands, Hugo released hers. He, too, had felt an emotion which he knew he had to suppress before it took root. Whilst the war raged, he had to keep his whole being focused on it.

Rose continued to busy herself around the

farm each day, aware as always that her mother avoided helping domestically. However, there was one person who received Flora's attention—Mrs Tabley. In Flora's eyes, the only two people of her generation with any class in the neighbourhood were the lady of the manor and herself. When newly married, she had thought it only natural that she and Mrs Tabley would be bosom friends, but despite Flora's most persistent endeavours, she was firmly excluded.

In the privacy of genteel drawing-rooms, Mrs Tabley would delicately shudder as she spoke of the eccentric woman who had enchanted Edward Edmunds into marriage.

Flora never trusted delivery of her remedies to anyone other than Rose and so on Monday afternoon, on hearing of Mrs Tabley's latest indisposition, a bottle of lavender water was hastily wrapped in tissue paper. Despite the fact that Rose was busy making jam, her mother insisted she went immediately to the manor. Knowing better than to argue with her mother, Rose set off briskly.

Thoughts of domestic matters were being inched away by her latest conversation with Hugo and she slowed down. Some of the village girls were already working in munitions factories or as domestics in the ever-growing number of hospitals which were needed for the constant flow of wounded. Should she do so, too? But what about the farm?

If she left, then her father and the others would have to work even harder and of late Edward seemed constantly tired, wearied by trying to make the utmost use of every inch of his land. Might her mother be persuaded, shamed even, into taking over some of Rose's responsibilities? Quickly she dismissed the thought. Anger swept over her. How could her mother be so detached from life when so much needed doing?

Stopping, she stared at the bottle of lavender water in her hand. Barney had often told her that his mother generally consigned Flora's lotion and potions to the rubbish heap, so what on earth was she doing now, going on such a worthless errand? With sudden determination, she began to retrace her steps, but then hesitated. When Flora sent her to the manor, she always questioned Rose about what she had seen and heard there.

A dog barked close by, no doubt one of the manor's large retrievers. Shading her eyes, she quickly scanned the surrounding fields.

'Rose, what luck! I needed to see you.'

Barney was running towards her across the field, the dog bounding along ahead of him. She sighed. There would be no quiet thinking now! Reaching her, Barney sharply silenced the dog, ordering him to stay a few feet away.

'Let me guess. You are going to my languishing mother with one of your mother's magic potions.'

25

'Actually I was thinking of turning back. Suddenly it all seemed such a waste of time.'

Reaching out, he touched the hand holding the bottle.

'I'll take it if you like. For once I think Mother might welcome it.'

'She really is in a state then?'

Rose clutched the bottle a little tighter. Perhaps she should go to the manor after all. There might be something she could do to help.

'She's now in the wicked-one phase, and going on about being all alone in the world.'

'Well, with you gone, I suppose she will be.'

'I've been wanting to talk to you about that. Rose, will you go and see her sometimes?'

'Barney, I really don't think I'm on your mother's social list.'

'Don't you see? That's what she'll need. Someone who'll come to see her because they care about her, not because they're part of the same social circle which is motivated by convention. You do care about her, don't you?' he asked with an anxiety which startled her.

'Of course I care about her. I'm not that hard-hearted,' she replied more sharply than she had intended.

'So you'll go then!'

'I didn't say that. I might have other plans.'

'What other plans?'

He seized her wrist and the suddenness of his action coupled with the pain made her cry

26

out.

'Barney, stop it! What's got into you?'

'Rose, I'm sorry. I wouldn't hurt you for the world,' he said, letting her go.

Then seeing his abject misery, she bit back her sharp words.

Instead she asked softly, 'What is it, Barney? There's something else, isn't there?'

'Rose, will you sit down a minute? I want to talk to you. How about sitting here?' he suggested, indicating a nearby moss-covered log.

They sat in silence, Rose caressing the dog who was now resting his head on her lap. She caught her breath as she saw the solemn set of Barney's face. Was he going to tell her that he was leaving immediately?

Although she had known he was intending to enlist, now it was imminent, she was gripped by fear. They had grown up together. It would be the end of their friendship for when he came back there would be no shared experiences. He would have seen such terrible things.

'Rose, will you marry me?'

Panic sent the blood pounding through her veins, and she prayed that she had misheard.

'I said, will you marry me?' Barney repeated.

This time there was no mistaking the urgency of his question. Forcing herself to meet his eyes, she was appalled to see . . . was

27

it panic?

'Rose, I love you. I want you to be my wife. Don't you understand?'

Looking away, she nodded imperceptibly. Although she did indeed understand what he had said, her thoughts were disjointed fragments. He had never mentioned love before. She liked him, but . . .

'I don't want to come back and find someone else has got you.'

'There isn't anyone else.'

'Then there's no problem,' he said jubilantly. 'We can get engaged before I go. Don't you see? I need to know you will still be here when I get back, someone to fight for.'

'There's your mother, the manor.'

'They're part of the past. I need to know there will be a future for me, with you. Thinking of you here, waiting for me, that will make enlisting seem all worthwhile. I'll be fighting for you, my Rose.'

Knowing from past experience that to keep pushing Rose might well frighten her away, Barney fell silent. Her panic giving way to cooler thinking, it was his last sentence which kept going round and round in her head.

I'll be fighting for you, my Rose.

He had always seemed so light-hearted about everything, never thinking about tomorrow. But then she had been like that, too. Now, for hundreds, perhaps thousands of men, there would be no tomorrow.

28

'Yes, I'll wait for you.'

'Promise?'

'I promise,' she replied quietly.

CHAPTER THREE

'So although you knew all about this, you said absolutely nothing to either Rose or me?' Flora asked, standing straight-backed in the musty parlour where Edward had called both her and Rose.

Rose shivered. When Flora was in such a mood she seemed like a snake coiled to strike and strike she did.

'Isn't it bad enough that I made a disastrous alliance without you agreeing to Rose doing the very same thing? And what arrogance that you didn't see fit to consult me about it!'

'I didn't see the need,' Edward replied calmly. 'Rose will be bettering herself, something of which you of all people would surely approve.'

Rose hated it when even the most seemingly innocent remark by her father was twisted to social standing by Flora. It was a hundred times worse when, like now, it was so close to home. Flora's downward move on the social ladder brought on by her marriage was a flash-point for so many subjects that Edward only spoke directly to her when necessary.

'Rose will never be allowed to forget she is not Mrs Tabley's equal. That woman will contrive it at every opportunity, but, oh, so subtly! It will be like a million pin pricks, far more damaging than a dagger's thrust of straightforward snobbishness,' Flora proclaimed.

'Mrs Tabley sounded most sincere when she said Rose would be the daughter she never had, living at the manor.'

'Living at the manor?' Rose and Flora chorused, united in shock.

'Barney never said anything about that,' Rose said, outraged. 'He just asked me to keep his mother company sometimes.'

Having found her voice, she rounded on her father whom she had always considered most honourable.

'And how dare you arrange my life without asking me!'

'If you would let me finish,' Edward said wearily. 'Rose, your happiness is very important to me and so I persuaded Mrs Tabley to agree that you will be here, at the farm, during the day, but will spend the evenings at the manor and sleep there. I thought you would understand that without Barney, his mother will be very lonely, frightened for his safety. Also, as one day you will be mistress of the manor, I saw no harm in you tasting a little of what life is like there.'

Mistress of the manor? Rose's spirit froze and sensing this Flora rounded on her.

'You hadn't thought of that, had you, when you agreed to this ridiculous marriage? What were you thinking about? I wouldn't have thought you silly enough to be carried away by some romantic dalliance with Barney.'

'If you hadn't been so wrapped up with those herbs of yours, you might have noticed more,' Edward accused coldly.

'And what about you? She's more your daughter than mine, you've seen to that, involving her in the farm almost as soon as she could walk.'

'Stop it, both of you!' Rose shrilled. 'Recriminations about the past solve nothing, and what you both seem to forget is that I'm an adult.'

'Not in the eyes of the law,' Flora interrupted with satisfaction. 'You can't get married without parental consent until you're twenty-one. Plenty of time for you to change your mind.'

'I've promised Barney I'll wait for him until this is all over, I will go to the manor to sleep. At least there'll be no unpleasant atmosphere there.'

'Rose, I beg you not to go!' Flora began. 'I just know . . .'

But then she stopped short. If Rose spent time alone with Mrs Tabley, then sooner or later the difference in their status would become painfully obvious. Then they would see how strong this so-called love was!

31

Suddenly feeling suffocated, wanting to be alone, Rose ran out of the parlour and across the farmyard. She had to get away from everyone, but she was not to escape so easily, for rounding the corner of the stables, she was nearly run down by Barney on his bicycle. Skidding on the cobbles, he just managed to keep his balance.

Then dropping the bicycle, he rushed out with, 'I've just heard about what happened at the inn when Jim and Andrew got blind drunk and went on the rampage. It was those two so-called sweethearts deserting them! They kept shouting that they had been through hell and back, that they had carried photographs of those two girls with them through the most terrible conditions, and for what? Only to be dropped when they were no longer whole men.'

Taking him by the hand, she led him like a child to the old cider orchard which had been one of their favourite haunts when they were small. Automatically she went towards the gnarled, old apple tree which they had climbed to hide from the world of adults. Dropping down on to her knees in the dappled shade, Rose pulled Barney down beside her. Too much was happening, too many disturbing incidents threatening to shatter the safe world she had known all her life.

It was Barney who broke the silence, his voice muffled but insistent.

'Promise me you'll be here for me, whatever happens.'

Knowing that he was thinking about the two village lads and how their sweethearts had deserted them, her heart skipped a beat.

'I'm going to fight for you, Rose, to keep you safe.'

Scrambling on to his knees, his dark eyes sparkled with ardour.

'There's your mother and the manor to fight for, too,' she repeated yet again, not wanting the responsibility of being his sole purpose for going to war and returning safely.

'The manor's been here for hundreds of years and doesn't need me to survive. But you need me, don't you, Rose?' he demanded.

Seeing the pleading in his eyes, she prayed none of her uncertainties were mirrored in hers. She shivered. What had happened to the boy she had grown up with? War! That's what had happened! A war which was touching everyone with its cruel, deadly shadow.

'Of course I'll wait for you, Barney.'

'Promise!' he urged.

She nodded, but realised he had to hear her actually say, 'I promise.'

Not noticing her reply was the merest of reluctant whispers, his wide smile pricked her conscience. Just one word from her meant so much to him. When he pulled her towards him, she steeled herself for a demanding kiss, but when his lips brushed hers there was nothing of the fire of the cornfield. It was as if he had put her on an unobtainable pedestal.

That evening, the tension at home was so unbearable that after she had finished helping with the milking, Rose made her escape. Her mother's slight, knowing smile was as disturbing as her father's repeating that all he wanted was a good life for his only daughter. She wanted to shout at him that she already had a good life at the farm but instead, she remained silent. What was the use of yet more words? It was rash, rushed words which had built a trap around her . . . her promise to Barney . . . her father agreeing she go to the manor.

With disjointed, troubling thoughts milling about in her head, she broke into a run as though to escape from them. Oblivious to the fact she was now on manor land, she ran across the meadow surrounding the small lake. Her breath was coming in hot, painful gasps, her heart hammering and she did not hear Hugo's anxious shout.

'Rose! Stop!'

Close to her now, he underlined his order by hooking a strong arm around her slim waist. She stumbled, but he pulled her to him.

'There now, it's all right,' he soothed, as though to a frightened child.

Fighting to regain her breath, it seemed the most natural thing in the world to lean her head against his chest. Still holding her, his face was hard with anger.

'Is it Barney?'

'No.'

It was the sound of her own voice which jerked her back to reality. Suddenly aware that she was leaning against Hugo, she pulled away, burning with embarrassment. Releasing her, Hugo turned slightly to give her the space, time to regain control. If it wasn't Barney who had precipitated her into such a heedless hurtle, then who, or what was responsible?

'Would it help to talk?' he asked, his voice full of concern.

'Talking won't help,' she said grimly.

'How about giving it a try? I promise not to say anything unless you want me to.'

'A promise, that's what started all of this,' she said quietly, head down.

Then taking a deep breath, she rushed out the facts . . . her promise to Barney . . . Mrs Tabley wanting her at the manor . . . her parents . . .

If she had glanced at Hugo she would have seen a wide variety of emotions sweep across his face, one or two of which would have astonished her—anger at the trap Barney had sprung on her, annoyance at the way Barney, Mrs Tabley and Flora were ordering Rose's life, but there was also a trace of biter hopelessness which was swiftly replaced by anger at himself. Rose was now out of his reach, but had she ever been within his reach?

35

The war, his work, his family—all of those had meant she was unobtainable.

'I've shocked you, haven't I?' she asked finally, aware of his silence.

'Do you really want my opinion?' he asked.

'Yes! No! I don't know!'

He had an almost overwhelming desire to touch her, to take her in his arms, but instead he turned away slightly so he could not see her.

'I think,' he began slowly, 'it would have taken a stony heart to refuse Barney. You knew about the village lads being let down, but could you talk to him when he's had a chance to calm down?'

'No!' she interrupted almost angrily. 'I promised. I couldn't break my word. Suppose something happened to him. I would never forgive myself.'

Hearing her voice break on the last word, he forgot she was promised to another. Taking her gently in his arms he felt a surge of bitter pleasure as she relaxed against him. Stroking her hair, he clamped his mouth shut. He longed to ask her just one question, but knew he could not, should not. Did she love Barney?

But without warning she had broken free from his light restraint and was running back towards the farm. He opened his mouth to shout at her to stop, but closed it on a whisper of her name. He watched until she was out of sight, then with a heavy sigh, turned to walk

36

back to his cottage. He had to accept that Rose had committed herself to Barney. She was a girl who would keep her word and he had to respect that, for he, too, was committed, bound in a different way by the war.

Using the back stairs, Rose knew which loudly-creaking tread to avoid. She managed to reach the haven of her room without either of her parents calling out to her. She tiptoed across the old, uneven floorboards to sit dejectedly on her bed.

Normally when troubled she was able to find the starting thread of the problem and unravel it to a solution, but not that evening. There were too many intertwined threads. Her promise to Barney was the tightest, the most constricting, binding her to him, no matter what. Being part of the same thread, Mrs Tabley and having to live partially at the manor could not be resolved separately, so Rose ignored this.

Her parents . . . she sighed sadly. She loved them both but as Flora had always distanced herself from Rose as a child, when she had reached adulthood, there was not the bond of sharing. Her trust in her father was shaken, for why had he seemingly schemed for her future without first consulting her?

However, there was another thread, one which she deliberately avoided. Hugo! If she let her thoughts wander for just a second, she could still feel his arms about her, the beat of his heart, the extraordinary comfort of being close to him. There was no way Barney going to war could be balanced with this attraction she very unexpectedly felt for Hugo. Men saw it their duty to fight; women's duty was to wait faithfully.

*   *   *

'Rose! Barney's here!'

It was early the following morning when her father's calls nearly made her drop the pails of still-warm milk she was carrying into the dairy. So early a visit must mean only one thing. He was leaving! Biting her lip, she placed the pails on the stone slab.

'Rose!'

Now Barney's voice was added to her father's.

'I haven't much time. I've got to be in Worcester by mid-morning. Rose, where are you?'

She froze. She didn't want to see Barney! But knowing her father was bound to come to the dairy, she had to find a hiding place where he would never think of looking. So after first checking there was no-one about, she slipped out to run swiftly to her mother's distilling room. She would be safe there, for no-one was allowed to so much as open the door without Flora's permission. The calls receded but Rose had only a moment to savour her relief, for her mother suddenly spoke her name softly from the table where she had been crumbling dried herbs.

'Rose, I won't give you away. But perhaps you would like to tell me why you're so obviously intent on avoiding Barney?'

'I couldn't bear to say goodbye.'

Avoiding bundles of herbs hanging from the low rafters, Flora came to take both of Rose's hands in hers, a rare gesture of affection.

'You don't love him, do you?'

In the strange intimacy of the distilling room, Rose's confession that she did not know slid out before she could stop it.

'I'm fond of him,' she continued slowly, before asking, 'But where is the dividing line between fondness and love?'

'Between a man and woman, there is no dividing line. There would be fewer unhappy couples if one or other of them hadn't mistaken fondness for love. I've learned that bitter fact the hard way.'

'So fondness can become a lifetime trap?'

'Not if you are brave enough to make your escape. Rose, although you might find this hard to believe, there's a lot more of me in you than is apparent. So I guess you have no more courage than I had.'

They were still holding hands, Rose's eyes glinting with tears at this unexpected but sad insight into her mother's feelings. They stood in silence, reluctant to break this new bond of understanding. With a catch in her voice, it was Rose who spoke first.

'I can't tell Barney. It would be cruel. Suppose something happened to him? I would never be able to rid myself of the thought that he had taken an unnecessary risk because I had let him down. As for the future, well, you and Father seem happy enough.'

'Enough is a funny word,' Flora replied slowly. 'It implies sufficiency. But who knows? If I had had the courage, Edward and I might have found real, fulfilling happiness with others. But then I wouldn't have had you as a daughter and that really would have been a tragedy!'

*   *   *

'What a pity Barney missed you,' Mrs Tabley said that evening as she and Rose sat down to dine at a highly-polished table resplendent with silver, porcelain and crystal.

Not wanting to lie, Rose looked down at her dish of soup and taking this as an sign that her future daughter-in-law was trying to control her emotions, Mrs Tabley did not pursue the subject. Instead she made a mental note to school Rose in the necessity of avoiding all emotional displays so in future she would not look down, but would look up with eyes undimmed by tears.

The meal was an ordeal, for Rose was well aware that Mrs Tabley watched her every move, eagle-eyed for the slightest breach of etiquette. Warned of this by her mother, Rose observed Mrs Tabley discreetly and with the help of an occasional eye or head movement from Seymour, the only male indoor servant now left, she acquitted herself well.

There were more courses than she was used to and as Mrs Tabley talked almost incessantly, the meal took as long as all the daily eating time in the farm put together! Coffee was taken in the small drawing-room, and here, Mrs Tabley held forth on the history of the manor and to ensure her pupil was paying attention, Rose was asked questions about what she had been told. When she failed to respond accurately about the manor's rôle in the Battle of Worcester in the Civil War, Mrs Tabley reprimanded her sharply.

Rose could not take anymore. Getting to her feet, she mumbled something about being tired, and fled, not caring she would have earned a black mark. But had she looked back she would have seen Mrs Tabley nodding sagely, convinced Rose had become overwhelmed by the weight of history which would one day be in her keeping. Such a reaction meant she had grasped the importance of being granted such a privileged life.

At the end of her first week at the manor,

Rose was just beginning to congratulate herself on being able to cope better with her split way of living, when two events occurred to prove her wrong. She was just putting on her boots by the back door, ready to go back to the farm, when Seymour brought her a letter. She knew it had to be from Barney, but smiled wryly as she realised she did not know his handwriting. Rose picked up her coat and went out into the yard to read it.

He appeared to be full of vague excitement about army life, but rumours of spies being rife, he, along with the rawest recruit, had been sternly warned not to give away any details which might be useful to the enemy. It wouldn't be long before their letters would be heavily censored officially, but when Rose reached the more personal paragraphs, she coloured, feeling strangely awkward, embarrassed.

It was as though she was reading words meant for someone else. She and Barney had not courted in the usual way, so to read words used between lovers brought home to her the full impact of her promise to him, reluctant though it had been. Rose hastily crushed the letter deep into her skirt pocket.

All that day Rose worked hard, succeeding in trying to appear normal although Barney's letter was like a heavy weight in her pocket. She did not look at it again until she was walking back to the manor. Stopping by an ancient oak, she took a deep breath. The sooner she became accustomed to him writing to her as a lover, the better. Although she took out the envelope, she did not remove the letter. She wasn't given long to ponder, however, for the church clock's faint striking had her running towards the manor. Mrs Tabley hated unpunctuality and the last thing Rose wanted was yet another lecture on the virtues essential for a lady! In her haste, she did not realise she had dropped Barney's letter.

'Oh, do hurry, miss!' the old cook urged as Rose came in. 'Annie's got your soap, water and clothes all laid out. You know how madam hates to be kept waiting and there's a guest tonight.'

Rose ran to the boot room to kick off her boots for it had been made plain to her that the floors of the manor were not to be sullied by mud or dust. Then running light-footed, she managed to reach the security of her room without being challenged by Mrs Tabley. Here, she quickly dropped her working clothes on the floor, then washed in the warm water already poured for her in the flower-sprigged china bowl. Hurriedly, she scrambled into her one and only suitable dress. Then hearing the gong, she could do little more than hastily push straying curls into place.

Then the second disturbing event of that day occurred! As Rose paused at the drawing-room door to try to compose herself, she heard a voice which made her catch her breath. Hugo!

'Rose, is that you? Do stop loitering about like a naughty child.'

Tight-lipped at being likened to a child, Rose entered the stuffy room with a purposeful stride which had Mrs Tabley sighing. Having stood up as soon as he was aware of Rose's presence, Hugo came towards her, hand outstretched.

'Miss Edmunds, how nice to see you!'

As though by mutual consent, their hands touched only briefly and although Rose knew Hugo was looking directly at her, she kept her eyes firmly fixed on the knot of his tie. Why was he calling her Miss Edmunds? Was it just drawing-room etiquette, or was it a reminder that she was now the future lady of the manor, no longer Rose of Good Pasture Farm?

'Rose, have you lost your tongue?' Mrs Tabley reprimanded sharply. Then turning to Hugo she confided in a whisper, 'Although the poor girl is doing very nicely in this unaccustomed way of life, there are occasions . . .'

Although she had lived in the manor for only a short time, there had been many instances when Rose had had to bite her tongue, but this particular insensitive remark and in front of Hugo had her turning on her heel. But she was swiftly stopped by Hugo's light hand on her arm.

'Miss Edmunds, you know so much about this lovely countryside. Am I wrong in thinking I saw a heron down by the lake this morning?'

The way he spoke, as though her opinion really mattered, made her look at him directly, the understanding in his eyes accompanied by a smile which said that Mrs Tabley wouldn't know a heron from a sparrow!

Such things being close to Rose's heart, she replied willingly, as they went in to dine. Soon, she and Hugo were engrossed in animated conversation. Although Mrs Tabley did not find it interesting, she nodded approvingly. The latest of farm happenings might not be polite dining-room conversation, but at least Rose was talking in a lively manner which was charming in a young girl.

There would be time enough to school her in the more sedate aspects of conversation. Mrs Tabley smiled with satisfaction. By the time dear, heroic Barney returned, she would be well on the way to moulding Rose into the perfect wife, and what was nearly as important, a compliant daughter-in-law.

CHAPTER FOUR

'I've had a letter from Barney, if you can call these heavily-censored few lines a letter,' Mrs

Tabley said one evening several weeks later, and from her glare, Rose knew something else had also fuelled her obvious disapproval and it was to do with her.

Brandishing a sheet of cheap writing paper, Mrs Tabley had swept into the imposing Victorian conservatory where Rose, needing something to do, was picking dead leaves off pot plants.

'The dear, brave boy says he hasn't heard from you for ages. Well, what have you to say for yourself?'

Still with her back to Mrs Tabley, guilt froze Rose. Barney had begged her to write frequently but somehow there never seemed to be the time. First there had been the completion of the harvest, then the jamming and preserving. Up to going to France, his letters had been full of the life they would have together once he was home. Panicking that she was being swept along by a fast-flowing current, Rose had not replied in similar vein, but had concentrated on farm and estate matters. Barney's letters became even more intense, questioning, demanding that she reiterate her promise to wait for him. This she did, but try as she might, she could not bring herself to pen words of love.

'Well?' Mrs Tabley repeated sternly. 'I thought you would be well aware of our duty to write regularly to our dear boys. After all, Barney is fighting for us, for the manor, for your future together.'

'I know.'

Rose's words were a whisper, and Mrs Tabley was just going to order Rose to speak up, when she noticed the glint of tears in her eyes. Much to the astonishment of them both, Mrs Tabley patted Rose's shoulder.

'There, child, I do understand how you feel. When Mr Tabley and I were parted when he had to go to London on business, I was totally bereft. You are obviously sensitive to the fact that your letters might well upset Barney, reminding him of the manor and of you. He has such plans.'

Rose ran from the conservatory lest Barney's mother should sense the confusion and guilt churning up in her.

As winter arrived with its long nights, rain and gales, the continual bad news from France, coupled with the grief of bereaved families and the return of the wounded, made it very hard to keep smiling, to think optimistically.

At the end of a long, wet, wearisome day, Rose frequently longed to stay at the farm surrounded by the warmth and comfort of her home. Despite all of its grand furniture, the manor was cheerless in winter. Every morning, as she crept out of her bedroom, Rose vowed that when she was mistress, there would be huge fires in every room in the manor.

Mrs Tabley became increasingly depressed.

She did little more than read a few pages of the latest novel whilst listening for the postman's bicycle bell. It raised her hopes that it might mean there was a letter from Barney. She had become so dispirited that she no longer sought to improve Rose.

'Shall we play cribbage?' Rose asked one evening.

'I think not. I haven't the energy. It's a pity your mother never saw fit to see you had pianoforte lessons. Music can be so soothing.'

'I never wanted them,' Rose replied. 'I preferred to help around the farm.'

'I shall arrange for you to have lessons, here on my own grand piano. I know the very person.'

Although Edward did not attend church regularly, on Sundays when possible, he kept farm work to the minimum. This meant Rose had more time at the manor and it was on the following Sunday afternoon that Mrs Tabley announced piano lessons would begin after lunch. Rose entered the drawing-room with barely concealed annoyance for she did not relish being treated like a child by Miss Price, the local music teacher.

'Rose, please don't look so miserable.'

With open-mouthed amazement, she looked across to where Hugo was standing by the piano! But Rose's amazement quickly changed to embarrassment. Hugo was the last person she wanted to witness her musical ineptitude.

'I'm sorry, Mrs Tabley shouldn't have put you to so much trouble.'

'It's no trouble. It will be a very pleasant diversion.'

To Rose's astonishment, that is indeed what it proved to be. Hugo struck the happy balance between introducing her to the basics and yet not making her feel she was no more than a child. When he guided her hands on the keyboard, and his skin touched hers, she felt every tiny nerve tingle with expectancy. The first time this happened, she held her breath, darting him a look of apprehension, but he was intent on talking about the simple tune in front of them. Swiftly, she chided herself. How silly to think he had experienced the same thing, too!

The lesson passed so swiftly that it surprised them both when Mrs Tabley swept in to enquire on Rose's progress.

'She's a good pupil,' Hugo said, standing up. 'Although it's difficult to be sure after just one lesson, I think she has a good ear for music.'

Still sitting at the piano, Rose was reluctant to join in.

'Well, child, are you glued to the stool?'

This sharp reprimand from Mrs Tabley brought Rose instantly to her feet.

'Mrs Tabley,' Hugo intervened, 'if you would give us just a few minutes, I would like to set Rose some scales and exercises to

49

practise.'

With a gracious nod, Mrs Tabley left, but with the stern reminder that afternoon tea would be served in the conservatory in ten minutes.

As Hugo explained to Rose what he wanted her to do before the next lesson in a week's time, he was trying to maintain a calm exterior. Did Rose really understand what life would be like for her in the manor, once Barney returned, he wondered. And when would be the right time to return to her the letter he had found under the oak tree? Its crumpled condition indicated that it was certainly not one she had cherished.

Although Rose continued to return happily to the farm every day, the highlight of the following weeks was her piano lesson with Hugo. She practised diligently, eager to please her patient teacher. The lessons were always followed by afternoon tea. In her usual way, Mrs Tabley gave Hugo little option but to stay. Although Rose looked forward to this, she often squirmed inwardly when Mrs Tabley persistently questioned Hugo about his writing. When Mrs Tabley suggested that she arrange an afternoon when he could read some of his writing, he declined sharply, then left hastily.

'How modest of him,' she said with an understanding smile. 'But I do feel he shouldn't hide himself away as he does. It must be hard for him to be away from literary circles, but perhaps they can be a distraction. But he mustn't feel there is no-one he can turn to.'

Heaving herself up from her chair, she seemed to have forgotten Rose.

'I shall go this very minute to write to the bookshop in Worcester and ask them to send me his latest book. When I can discuss it with him, he will understand that I am truly interested,' she muttered.

It was early afternoon later that week when her father came to Rose carrying a full basket covered with a white cloth.

'Rose, as there isn't all that much to do today, will you take these supplies to Mr Smith? He hasn't been to the farm recently and I wondered if he was ill.'

'He was fine on Sunday,' Rose replied quickly, reluctant to go to Hugo's home. 'Perhaps it's more convenient for him to buy from the village.'

'I don't think so. He told me he didn't like the way everyone there seemed intent on questioning him. He laughed when I said a German spy wouldn't last two minutes there. So be a good girl and take this. It isn't much of a detour on your way back to the manor.'

As soon as she was out of sight of the farm, Rose slowed to a dawdle. She allowed her thoughts to wander and in a moment of great clarity, realised she avoided looking ahead.

51

There was always the niggling thought that there would be a letter from Barney. She always fled from his mother's eagle eye to read them, for they always reduced her to tears of hopelessness. She had heard enough from soldiers returning from the front to picture the terrible conditions and this filled her full of pity for the boy, now a man, who had been her childhood companion and who had never really had to face any unpleasantness, other than his mother's wrath.

But the words which really tormented her were his plans for the future with her. At first he expressed these in a buoyant, almost joking fashion, but then the tone had changed to a desperate uncertainty. Repeatedly he wrote that she was his anchor, his sole purpose in keeping alive.

As these thoughts milled around, tears welled up in Rose's eyes and she wiped them away. How could she cry merely for the muddle her emotions were in when others were crying from the true sorrow of bereavement? Quickening her step, she hurried towards the cottage by the lake, eager to get to the manor and try to write more lovingly to Barney.

Although Hugo's cottage was set in a garden, this had been overrun by weeds. Opening the garden gate, Rose could see Hugo sitting inside at a table by the small window, head bent low to make the most of the mellow light from an oil lamp. Knocking lightly on the door, she stood back and saw Hugo hastily gathering papers as he jumped up. She heard a drawer slam shut and then he was opening the front door, his unshaven face set.

'I've brought you these,' she rushed out, thrusting the basket towards him. 'Father thought you might be in need of milk and things.'

Although his face lightened, his smile did not reach his eyes.

'Rose, how kind of you both. I've been so busy, I quite forget.'

'Have you nearly finished your book then?'

'Do you want the basket back now?' he asked, evading her question.

'No, no, it will do the next time you go to the farm,' she replied.

'I won't keep you then. Thank your father for me.'

Astonished by his unwelcoming, brusque manner, she was startled to see him tug the curtains across the window. Were all writers this jumpy about their work, not wanting people to even glimpse the paper it was written on?

Hurrying to the manor, Rose shrugged off Hugo's odd behaviour for she was intent on composing the sort of letter she knew Barney wanted. As she opened the kitchen door, a tide of excited voices engulfed her.

'It's all very well madam going patriotic like, but we'll never all crowd into Dower Cottage,' Annie was worrying. 'Mind you,' she added with a smile, 'Mrs Peters handing in her notice like that will mean we'll have more room. You should have seen madam's face when she packed her bags and left. I heard her say that no enemy on earth would see her in a cottage, especially when she had had a better offer from a really high-class establishment.'

'Would someone please tell me what's happened?' Rose demanded, bending to take off her muddy boots.

'Madam has decided to turn the manor over to the authorities for a convalescent hospital,' Seymour said wearily.

Since Mrs Tabley had conceived the idea that morning, she had been writing numerous letters which he had had to post immediately. Then she had gone from room to room deciding what furniture to take with her to Dower Cottage. With Mrs Peters now gone, Seymour had been given the job of following with pad and pencil.

'What a good idea,' Rose said, sinking wearily down on to the old settle.

'But Dower Cottage hasn't been lived in for years, not since Barney's grandmother died when he was little,' Seymour replied.

They were interrupted by the very unusual sight of Mrs Tabley entering the kitchen.

'There you are, Rose! This isn't the time to

sit about idly. I want you to come with me and make a detailed inventory of everything I intend storing in the attics. We will begin in the drawing-room.'

Mrs Tabley had lost her usual indolence almost overnight and when Rose returned each evening she was always greeted with an update on what had happened that day from one or other of the servants. Officials and army officers were soon inspecting the manor for suitability. So eager were the authorities to have possession of the manor that they offered to move what was needed to Dower Cottage and so it was that Rose was again trailing after Mrs Tabley, though this time through what was to be their new home.

'Now, Rose, we mustn't let our standards drop, so although it will cramp this small drawing-room, we must bring the grand piano. You must continue your lessons for when this dreadful war ends and Society returns to normal. You must be ready to join it.'

Pausing to look reflectively at Rose in her serviceable skirt and blouse, Mrs Tabley added, 'I know we must all make sacrifices, but when we're settled here I must get my dressmaker to do something about the dire state of your wardrobe. I've a few good gowns that could be altered.'

'May I come in?' a voice interrupted.

Hugo had been on his way to the manor to offer help but, seeing the governess cart outside Dower Cottage, he guessed Mrs Tabley would be there, with, he hoped, Rose. Although their Sunday music lessons had carried on, they were constantly interrupted by the officers and Mrs Tabley twittering after them. He now waited to be bidden to enter the cottage drawing-room. He was well aware that Mrs Tabley had very fixed ideas about behaviour, social etiquette and he did not want to be shown to be lacking in that respect in front of Rose.

'Our literary gentleman! Do come in!' Mrs Tabley enthused. 'Rose and I are trying to come to terms with our new humble abode. But then we must all make sacrifices, mustn't we?'

To Rose's surprise, Hugo looked uncomfortable and seemed to be avoiding looking at either of them, but Mrs Tabley went prattling on about the manor's new rôle as a hospital, much of which Hugo already knew, as indeed did everyone in the village.

'I've brought Rose some new music,' Hugo broke in. 'I've just received it from London. But perhaps when you move here, it will not be convenient to continue with the lessons.'

'Of course you must continue with Rose's education. We must not let this dreadful war stop our lives completely and besides she will learn far more quickly without the distraction of Barney. You know how giddy a young girl in love can be,' she added.

56

Rose and Hugo exchanged quick glances, hers of anger at being classed as giddy, his thoughtfully quizzical. Rose was certainly not giddy, but was she truly in love? When she spoke about the farm and countryside she did so with a passion which sparkled in her eyes. This passion was beginning to show, too, in her piano playing. But she never spoke of Barney and still he had the letter.

'Thank you for the music,' Rose said hurriedly, holding out her hand, then opening the pages she frowned. 'Oh, it's the Chopin you played the other day from memory! It's much too difficult. I can't possibly play it.'

'Yes, you can,' Hugo said. 'I've told you before, you've great ability.'

Then seeing that Mrs Tabley had turned away to examine the freshly-hung curtains, he took Rose's hand in his, turning it palm upwards.

'People think a good pianist should have long, slender fingers but ability is more than just the hands.'

In the course of the lessons they had touched fleetingly, but now there was something in Hugo's voice. Although he was only cupping her hand, it suddenly seemed to Rose to be a caress.

'That's just as well,' she said awkwardly, almost snatching her hand away. 'Mine are so used to handling pitchforks that they're as hard as nails.'

'Oh, please!' Mrs Tabley interrupted. 'Farmyard matters are hardly the subject for polite conversation. If it wasn't for this terrible war, I would insist that Rose stopped working at the farm, it's so coarsening.'

'Are you saying I'm coarse?' Rose asked icily. 'If so I'll go back to where I belong.'

She moved with such rapidity that she was out of the room before either Mrs Tabley or Hugo could even think of any calming words. The sound of the front door slamming jerked Hugo into action. He caught up with Rose as she began to run across the meadow. He grabbed her arm. She would have fallen had he not swiftly encircled her waist with an unyielding arm.

'Rose, she didn't mean it!'

'Oh, but she did!' she exclaimed. 'I'm sick to death of her sly digs. My family might not be grand but we have our pride.'

'Rose! Dear Rose! Stop it!' he ordered gently.

It wasn't his words which stopped her tirade but the understanding she saw in his face. Suddenly she was crying, and when he guided her head to his shoulder she did not resist.

'Is it really that bad?' he asked finally. 'To be brutally frank, she won't live for ever and then you will be mistress of the manor.'

'I don't want to be mistress of the manor.'

A glimmer of hope had Hugo daring to ask, 'And what about Barney? He might not want to leave his ancestral home.'

For several seconds which seemed to Hugo as long as eternity, Rose said nothing. Then putting her hands on his chest she levered herself away, but only by a few inches.

'Do you believe in fate?' she asked. 'Are all the major events in our lives preordained?'

'When it comes to war, it's man's folly.'

'But in other things, personal things.'

'Relationships, you mean? I just don't know. As we go through life we come across so many instances when we have to decide on the path we take. Is that really free will, or only a pretence? You're thinking about Barney, aren't you? Is it meant to be that you and he . . .'

'Don't!'

Turning away from him, she covered her face with her hands.

He thought he heard her whisper, 'What have I done?'

'Rose, dearest Rose.'

Half-turning, she ordered harshly, 'Don't call me that. It isn't right!'

Then she was away across the field as though trying to escape from something dreadful.

That night, Hugo decided, he would burn the letter he had found under the oak tree.

Rose still had not quite regained her composure by the time she returned to Dower Cottage. Glancing up and seeing Mrs Tabley's bedroom curtains were closed, she realised her action must have brought on one of Mrs Tabley's turns. Her relief that she would be free for the rest of the day was tempered by a sense of guilt.

She was just going to walk around to the kitchen door when she heard someone coming along the gravel path. Turning, and seeing a soldier in uniform pushing a bicycle, she knew instinctively it had something to do with Barney. Every word of what had just passed between her and Hugo was still crystal clear in her mind and guilt hit her even harder.

'Miss, are you all right? Sorry if I scared you.'

Hurriedly leaning his bicycle against the house wall, the soldier hesitated, wondering whether to put a comforting hand on her arm. But from Barney's description, he knew this was Rose Edmunds and a private did not get familiar with an officer's lady.

'He's all right, the lieutenant's OK,' he rushed on. 'He knew I was coming on leave and as it's only a short bike ride from where I live, he asked me to bring you this.'

Fumbling in his pocket, the soldier drew out what looked like a small knot of khaki material. Swallowing hard, Rose took it, but made no attempt to examine it. Then aware of the awkward silence, she forced a smile as she invited him in for a cup of tea.

'No thanks, miss. I'd better be getting back.

I've two nippers, you see and want to spend as much time as I can with them.'

She watched him go, her fist clenched tightly around what he had brought from Barney. Then, taking a deep breath, she pulled away the matcrial. When Barney's signet ring was revealed, she stared at it with a mixture of horror and fright. There was no note, but she knew he expected her to wear it. She glanced at the wedding-ring finger on her left hand but then hurriedly tried the ring on her right hand. Relieved when this proved to be too small, she decided to wear the ring on a ribbon around her neck. This would fulfil what Barney intended, but it would not be visible to others.

CHAPTER FIVE

On the second Friday in December the manor was turned over to the military and the move to Dower Cottage accomplished. It all happened so swiftly that Rose and the servants were in a daze, but not Mrs Tabley.

Still in the afterglow of having made a great sacrifice, she continued to organise everyone else in the household, but now from the comfort of her favourite chair in the drawing-room.

On Saturday, as the domestic side of the convalescent hospital was not yet functional,

Rose was sent to offer the officers hospitality. As usual she went in through the kitchen of the manor, now cold and silent. She hurried through to the hall, hearing voices from upstairs. She called out.

'Dawson, go and see who that is,' an impatient loud voice ordered. 'If it's that awful, pretentious Tabley woman, get rid of her.'

Although Rose hated the way Mrs Tabley often talked to her, her mouth clamped in a straight line at this description coming from the one to whom the manor had been turned over. She was on the point of marching away when someone came hurtling down the stairs.

'He didn't mean it, you know,' a young, fresh-faced captain explained.

'Mrs Tabley needn't have handed over the manor,' Rose replied icily.

'I know, I'm sorry, but we're all rushed off our feet and the colonel is tetchy at the best of times. We really are very grateful to Mrs Tabley but it has to be made plain to her we now . . . er . . .'

He trailed off under Rose's steady gaze. But she wasn't looking at him in a defiant manner. There was something about this young officer which reminded her of Barney. Their colouring was the same, their build, and when the captain ran his fingers through his hair like Barney used to do when embarrassed, she felt the need to ease his obvious tension.

'You're in charge here?' she finished helpfully, head to one side.

She tried to put him at his ease.

'We . . . Mrs Tabley, that is, was wondering if you would like to come over to Dower Cottage for lunch tomorrow.'

'Just me?' William Dawson replied, hardly able to believe his good luck.

'No, the colonel as well and of course the other officers,' she added awkwardly.

Mrs Tabley had been very firm that her offer did not extend to other lesser ranks!

'Hang on a minute while I go and check.'

Rose moved away to peep into the various rooms where beds were already lined up against walls. The thought of the injured soldiers who would soon occupy them brought the trickle of tears to her eyes, her hand going to where Barney's ring hung suspended on white ribbon. As the captain began coming down the stairs and saw her standing there with drooping shoulders, he thought she, like so many others, had experienced personal war-inflicted tragedy. Quietly, he continued down, coming to stand just beside her.

'You'll all come then?' she asked.

'Yes, we would be very grateful. Will it be all right if we let you know exact numbers this afternoon? Men come and go.' Then seeing her nod, he added awkwardly, 'I'll see you later then.'

That night, lying in her smaller bedroom,

Rose felt physically and mentally battered. Mrs Tabley had seemed almost childishly excited at the thought of entertaining the officers from the manor and had the servants rummaging in various tea chests for the best china, glasses and table linen.

Although Rose knew her father and mother would be delighted if she stayed for the evening meal at the farm, something held her back from asking. At Dower Cottage, so much was happening she hadn't five minutes to be by herself, to think, be calm, and it was what she needed.

This very desperation cleared her thoughts so she was able to come up with a plan which would give her a few hours' freedom. Mrs Tabley knew nothing about farm work so Rose would have no problem in coming up with some excuse which meant she had to stay late to help. But what to do during the intervening hours?

Then she remembered the small, wooden shed by the lake where the water bailiffs had once stored their various tools and equipment. She had no trouble in working out how to smuggle bread, cheese and milk from the farm. After all she had done this often enough as a child!

Keeping to hedge shadows in the moon-lit fields, Rose moved at a steady, but cautious pace. It was with a feeling of relief that she pushed open the dilapidated door of the boat house. Slipping inside, she left the door open, hoping that in the moonlight she would be able to find something to sit on. Besides, it would be good to look out on the moon-dappled water whilst she ate.

Her simple supper consumed, thoughts drifted to many happy occasions when, either with Barney or by herself, she had enjoyed similar feasts. But what Rose had not considered was the cold night air that began to seep through her coat. Rising, she hunched her shoulders, hands thrust deep into her coat pockets. It was far too early to go back to Dower Cottage, for the kitchen would still be bustling with activity and she would not be able to go unseen up the back stair.

Perhaps the lakeside shed hadn't been such a good idea after all! Through the wind-whipped branches of the willows she could just glimpse the wavering light from the kitchen of Dower Cottage. When that went out, she would hurry to its welcoming warmth. Meanwhile she would walk briskly around the lake, checking the lights at Dower Cottage on each circuit.

Rose had forgotten that what had once been a narrow but well-defined path had now been partially reclaimed by brambles. She had only taken a few steps before they were snatching at her coat. What she had intended to be a quick walk turned into a slow affair as she frequently bent to disentangle the brambles.

Pausing to suck painful thorns out of her hands, she was entranced by the sheer magic of the still water mirroring the full moon. Clenching her fists, her imagination flashed pictures of what it might be like on the battlefields, with the same moon, trees leafless. Was Barney trying to sleep in some waterlogged trench? Was he also looking up at the same moon, thinking of the manor, perhaps of her?

Suddenly, as though escaping from a nightmare, she turned and began to run, heedless of the brambles tugging at her coat. She was heedless, too, of danger and as her foot hooked under a low, tangled arch of brambles, she fell. She cried out in fright, but as her hands touched the cold, moist soil, she broke into pitiful sobbing. This must be what it was like to lie injured in the cold mud of France. When a hand touched her shoulder, she screamed.

'Rose, it's me!' a deep voice said as she was hauled roughly to her feet.

'Hugo?' Rose whispered, unsure.

'What on earth are you doing here? Have you been crying? Is it bad news about Barney?'

'No, I'm just cold.'

'It's a good job I haven't damped the fire down for the night. The kettle should still be hot.'

Without another word, he took her hand and walked so quickly towards his cottage that she broke into a stumbling trot. She made no attempt to remove her hand until they were standing in his kitchen, but then as the glow from the oil lamp made this physical contact visible, she hastily pulled away.

'Go and sit by the fire,' he said. 'I'm thinking you need to get warm. Sit by the fire and I'll make us a brew. Let me have your coat and I'll try to get the mud off before Mrs Tabley sees it. Or was it her you were running away from?' he added sharply.

With unnecessary concentration she undid the coat buttons and still with downcast eyes, handed it to him.

'Dear Rose,' he said softly, dropping the coat over a chair back. 'What is it? What had you running around the lake at this time of night?'

Gently cupping her chin, he tipped her face up so she had no option but to look at him.

'You saw me?'

She flushed as much from the touch of his hand as from the room's heat.

'I like to take a walk on moonlit nights. Now, if Barney is all right and Mrs Tabley wasn't chasing you, though I can't imagine her doing anything so undignified, what is wrong?'

'Nothing . . . oh, everything!' she blurted out.

'I'm a good listener,' he said, leading her to a sagging but comfortable fireside chair. 'I'll make that tea. It might help.'

Whilst he busied himself, she sat motionless, gazing into the fire until her eyes seemed to dry from the heat. Handing her a mug of tea, Hugo then sat opposite her. As she sipped the sweet, warming liquid, he did not press her to talk, but watched discreetly. When she did begin to speak, it came almost as much as a surprise to her as to him.

'Do you ever feel so confused that you seem a stranger to yourself?'

'Frequently, especially these days. This dreadful war hurls everyday life into such confusion.'

'Do you really think so?' she asked softly.

'It's only natural to worry about loved ones.'

She shook her head slowly, her face a neutral mask. This told Hugo as surely as though she had spoken that Rose was unsure about her love for Barney. But he said nothing as he fought the urge to take her in his arms. Abruptly he stood up, going to a dresser drawer to rummage for a clothes brush. With more vigour than was needed he brushed her coat, his back to her so she should not see the brightness of hope in his eyes. But this did not last long as with shame he remembered Barney. Barney was at the front, fighting for her, and indirectly for him.

'I'd better be going. Thank you,' she was saying.

With silent formality he helped her on with her coat, then went to open the door. As she went to pass him, she paused to looked up at him.

'Life does get into a tangle, doesn't it?'

'It can sometimes be untangled,' he said softly.

'Promises can't be untangled.'

'They can if both parties are willing,' he said, hoping he hadn't sounded too eager.

She said nothing, the slight shake of her head telling him that she knew Barney would not be willing. And who could blame him? Rose really was a girl in a million.

*   *   *

The Christmas season was not heralded with excited planning. There were too many heavy hearts for that. However, at the manor, now full of wounded officers, Mrs Tabley took it upon herself to organise things to cheer the patients, although it was Rose who had to do all the work! When he could, Captain William Dawson helped, but knowing now of her relationship to Barney, he treated her with gentle concern.

An impressive Christmas tree was felled on the estate and brought into the hall and patients who were able were cajoled into making decorations for it. Fir cones gathered by Rose were secured on ribbon or string, streamers cut from scraps of coloured paper were festooned from the branches and from

Good Pasture Farm, Madge sent twists of paper containing toffee and fudge. Flora's small, pretty lavender bags added an extra, if unseasonal, scent to the tree.

As Rose had dreaded might happen, the very first patient had barely been made comfortable before her mother arrived at the manor clutching an assortment of her herbal remedies. It was William Dawson, unfortunately not knowing of their relationship, who told Rose about Flora marching purposefully into the drawing-room ward where she tried to dose patients. To William's credit, he described the ensuing scene with such gentle humour that Rose laughed, not at her mother, but at the following chaos.

It was only later he discovered that Flora was Rose's mother. He and Rose were sitting on the stairs twining ivy around the oak spindles of the banisters when he tried to stammer out an apology. Turning around, Rose laughingly told him she had not taken his light-hearted report amiss. Relieved, William bent forward, touching her shoulder in a gesture of gratitude. Perhaps because this was so like Barney, she briefly covered his hand with hers.

Although this scene lasted only seconds, it was what Hugo saw as he entered the hall, carrying a box of books which had arrived from London. Although he had been to the manor a couple of times to entertain patients by playing popular tunes, he had not especially picked out William Dawson from the rest of the officers. But now, seeing him and Rose so close, friendly, Hugo's jaw hardened. Had Rose, too, seen his similarity to Barney? And if so, had this drawn her to the captain, despite what she had hinted about her promise to Barney?

Hugo was filled with an emotion he did not recognise then, but did shamefacedly later—jealousy!

'Hello, Hugo!'

Running down the stairs towards him it was Rose herself who brought his thoughts back to normal.

'What have you got there?' she asked with the delightful excitement.

'Books,' he replied shortly, dumping his load on to an empty chair.

'Good! Some of the patients are well enough to read, but unfortunately Mrs Tabley had every book from the library here hidden away. Shall we hand them out now?'

Relieved she had forgotten her previous task of helping the captain, Hugo matched her eagerness, a very willing porter, as she ran from bed to bed handing out the books.

'Miss Edmunds, no running in the ward, if you please!'

This sharp order brought Rose to a halt and although she was not facing him, Hugo could tell from the set of her shoulders that this was not the first time this particular nursing sister had berated Rose. Hiding his anger, Hugo apologised swiftly.

'I'm sorry, Sister, it's my fault. I should have checked with you first.'

Sister Kate Clark softened.

'Thank you, I would appreciate that.' She smiled. 'But anyway it is nearly time for the evening meal.'

'Evening meal!' Rose exclaimed, thrusting the book she was holding back into the nearly empty box. 'I hadn't realised the time.'

'If you're late, will Mrs Tabley send you to bed with just bread and cheese?' Hugo teased, following her as she rushed to fetch her coat.

'It's no laughing matter!' Rose gasped. 'I seem to be getting a lot of black marks from everyone just lately . . . Mrs Tabley . . . that nursing sister.'

She rushed out of the front door.

'Rose, stop! It's cold out there! Do up your buttons,' he ordered, catching her by the arm. 'Here, let me.'

'You sound just like my granny when I was little,' she half complained, half laughed, though she did indeed stop, but as he began to fasten her buttons, the intimacy of his action flooded her cheeks with crimson.

'I can manage,' she said, hastily fumbling with the top button.

'Sorry. I shouldn't have . . .'

'It's all right,' she flung over her shoulder as she hurried away.

Catching her up, he said softly, 'I'll see you back to Dower Cottage.'

Hugo fell into step beside her as they walked down the laurel-edged path to Dower Cottage. When she stumbled, Hugo grabbed her hand. When she did not remove it, he gently threaded her arm through his. Such a closeness silenced both of them and although they did not know it, they both shared the same thought—how companionable it was. Then as though by mutual consent, when they were in sight of Dower Cottage, they moved apart, their farewells loud, as though to dispel any questioning thoughts listeners might have. Hugo had only been escorting Rose out of polite courtesy.

When Rose began dressing on Christmas morning, she was just about to tie the ribbon with Barney's signet ring around her neck, when she stopped. She had the sudden, oddest idea that wearing it would prevent her and others having a happy time. Although knowing Barney would be having a miserable Christmas in awful conditions, she had an overpowering urge to be free of him, just for a few hours. Just for Christmas Day, she wouldn't wear his ring next to her skin.

Barney wouldn't know, it wouldn't make any difference to him. Hurriedly thrusting the ribbon and ring into the small rosewood box holding her few pieces of modest jewellery, Rose locked it. Like a guilty child not wanting to be caught out in a bad act, she hid the key behind a china shepherdess on the mantelpiece.

Then turning to a chair, Rose carefully gathered up the dress her mother had given her for Christmas. Wanting to enhance the beauty she knew lurked under Rose's normally workaday clothes, Flora had chosen a deep-pink, lace-ruffled dress. Feeling a little like Cinderella, Rose put on the pretty gown, but as she twirled in front of the full-length mirror, her bottom lip trembled. Although she had spent Christmas Eve at the farm, this was the first Christmas Day she would not be seeing her parents, but Mrs Tabley had been adamant that Rose should be with her, a comfort to make up for Barney's absence.

Going down to breakfast, Rose was astonished to see Mrs Tabley sitting at the table, her puffed eyes indicating that she had been weeping. Rose did something she had never done before. She brushed a kiss on the older woman's cheek. To Rose's surprise, she was seized in a tight embrace.

'Rose, dear Rose! What would I do without you, though of course you are no substitute for my own darling child. Unlike me, you're so brave, no sign of tears which is as it should be for someone destined to marry a hero.'

As Mrs Tabley's sobs turned to a wail,

Annie produced a glass of brandy.

'Here, madam, drink this,' she said firmly, as Rose managed to free herself. 'You know a little medicinal brandy always helps.'

Rose raised her eyebrows for Annie had poured a very generous measure! Mrs Tabley appeared not to notice this and between juddering sobs, she downed it in a few gulps.

'There now, madam, let's get you up to bed. A nice rest before you go out is what you need. Perhaps Miss Rose will help us.'

After they had partially undressed their drink-sleepy charge, Rose and Annie tiptoed downstairs.

'Do you normally give her that much?' Rose asked.

'No, but I reckoned all of us deserved some peace today. Madam will sleep soundly until this evening when we serve Christmas dinner. By then she won't be feeling so badly about Mr Barney not being here. So you see, I'm thinking of her, too!'

As Annie hurried to fetch hotter coffee for the dining-room, there was a knock on the front door and Rose opened it to see William Dawson.

'Happy Christmas, Miss Edmunds. I hope you will not think me forward, but I've brought you a little gift.'

Thrusting a small box into her hand, he rushed away before Rose could do more than call out her thanks. She was just about to close the door when another visitor arrived, Hugo. Like a naughty child she hurriedly pushed William's gift under a scarf on the hallstand.

'Was that the captain I saw leaving?'

His cold question cut across Rose's seasonal greeting and she replied in a similar tone.

'Yes, it was, but I can't see why our visitors should be of so much interest to you.'

'Rose, I'm sorry, it really is none of my business,' he apologised, but a little voice inside him insisted that it was his business.

There was Barney and now the captain. It was said women were captivated by men in uniform. Seeing him standing there seemingly lost for words, cold, dejected, Rose's annoyance was swept away by concern.

'Come in,' she invited. 'I doubt you've had a proper breakfast and Cook always makes more than enough.'

'Mrs Tabley?'

His question hung in the air, an acknowledgement that she would not approve of such an intimate meal.

'Oh, she's sleeping off a generous amount of brandy, purely medicinal of course,' she added with a smile.

As he took off his overcoat and hung it on the hallstand, Rose caught her breath. Suppose he saw William's gift? But taking a small flat parcel out of his pocket, he handed it to her, begging her not to open it until he had gone.

'In that case I had better take it up to my room, for if Mrs Tabley sees it, she will insist I open it then and there. You go on into the dining-room. I'll only be a minute.'

Hurrying up to her room, Rose went to her suitcase on top of the wardrobe and from this hiding place she took out a small, round-lidded box made of plaited straw.

During the last few days she had been helping in the farm kitchen and had managed to squirrel away toffee, small cakes, biscuits and a jar of quince preserve and one of green tomato chutney. She thought Madge hadn't noticed, but just as Rose was leaving with coat pockets bulging with her hoard, Madge had handed her the straw box.

'If you put that lot in here it will make a better gift,' she said dryly. 'I don't want to know who it's for, but if you think he needs such things, that's good enough for me.'

Now, running down the stairs with her gift for Hugo, Rose saw Annie coming through the door from the kitchen.

'There'll be two for breakfast, Annie, and no, Mrs Tabley hasn't made a miraculous recovery!'

When the maid told Seymour and Cook it was Hugo who was breakfasting with Miss Rose, they both tut-tutted at such goings-on. When Annie remarked blithely that there was no harm in breakfast, it was supper which could lead to the bedroom, the two older

77

servants looked aghast. Then Annie had the temerity to order them not to tell Mrs Tabley about the unexpected breakfast guest.

CHAPTER SIX

Although Annie had seen nothing wrong in Hugo and Rose breakfasting together, nevertheless she did not leave them alone. But even though chaperoned, Hugo thought how pleasant it was to have Rose sitting across a table, smiling, tending to his needs as she told him about previous Christmases at the farm.

Occasionally he caught just a hint of sadness as she realised that such homely, comparatively simple celebrations would never be hers again. He, too, was remembering other happy Christmases, but spent in another country about which he neither wanted, nor could not, talk about. And yet if it had been possible, it was with Rose he would want to recapture the past, but she was promised to another.

Hurriedly he rushed out yet more thanks for his unusual gift. That she had prepared it herself gave it added meaning. But, he pulled himself up sharply, perhaps this was the custom in farming communities where neither shops nor an abundance of money made purchasing gifts usual.

Guilt now swamped him. What was he doing enjoying such a meal with another man's intended bride, especially when that man was standing knee-deep in icy water in a rat-infested trench? Hurriedly draining the last of his coffee, he was already pushing his chair away from the table when Seymour burst into the dining-room, obviously anxious.

'Excuse me, Miss Rose, but Annie must hurry to madam's room. She's ringing so furiously that the bell on the kitchen wall is threatening to break from its moorings.'

As Annie muttered, 'She's never come to this fast before!' both Rose and Hugo wondered if the brandy was the normal cure for Mrs Tabley's turns.

Voicing his thanks for the meal, he announced he had better be going. That, coupled with the servants scurrying, had Rose standing with a hand to her head. One minute everything was calm, relaxed, enjoyable, the next, chaos! Seymour, having quickly regained his composure, was once more intent on seeing life went according to plan.

'Miss Rose, might I remind you that you were to accompany madam when she visited the wounded at the hospital this morning? If you'll pardon me for saying so, madam will see it as a duty that you now go in her stead.'

So after enquiring about Mrs Tabley and receiving an assurance that she was, as Annie put it, still a little mazed, Rose reluctantly prepared to go. But she had no intention of being the substitute for the Lady of the Manor. She knew it was a rôle with which she would never be comfortable.

'May I walk with you?'

In the confusion, Rose had forgotten Hugo was still standing in the hall. 'Hugo, I'm sorry! What must you think of me leaving you like that?'

'It doesn't matter! I've been admiring these miniatures of previous occupiers of the manor. I see there's one of the present Mrs Tabley.'

They exchanged glances of sad resignation, for one day Rose would be there, too.

Because many of the villagers were calling with small gifts or just to visit the wounded, the front door of the manor had been left ajar and entering the hall, Rose and Hugo were met by unexpected loud laughter and cheering. To their astonishment, a hectic wheel-chair race was in progress but as wheel-chairs ricocheted off the ancient panelling, Rose winced.

'It's a good thing our esteemed lady of the manor can't see this,' Hugo murmured.

'Do you think I should have a word?'

Rose worried, for even though she often felt constrained by Mrs Tabley's unbending attitude, nevertheless she had come to love the old house. But Hugo shook his head.

'No, don't say anything. These men have gone through so much. If it wasn't for them, who knows what would happen to this country. I feel . . .' but he was interrupted by a woman's commanding voice above the noise.

'Hugo, the very man! We need someone to play carols for us.'

Standing on tiptoe, Rose saw Sister Kate Clark threading her way through the wheel-chairs. Surprised she was using Hugo's Christian name, Rose was relieved to see Kate Clark had lost her severe manner. It was, though, soon obvious that Kate's smile had been solely for Hugo.

Reaching him and seeing his companion, she asked coldly, 'Not busy mucking out cow byres today then?'

'No, but it's a job which has to be done, like emptying bedpans,' Rose retorted swiftly.

Standing between two stony-faced women, Hugo hurriedly said he would go and play the battered old piano which had been brought down from the nursery.

'You seem to be gathering quite a collection of notable men,' Kate Clark spoke softly. 'Are you hedging your bets in case Barney Tabley doesn't return? But let me tell you, you would find it just as difficult to fit in with Hugo's literary friends as with the manor set. The first would need intellect, the second, good breeding.'

Rose was well used to sharp-tongued local women, but the sister's cutting remarks shocked her into silence. Satisfied that her barbed comments had found their target, Kate Clark went to stand close to Hugo, ostensibly to lead the singing. Tight-jawed with anger, Rose turned to leave, but someone else had heard the remarks—William Dawson.

'Miss Edmunds!'

He stopped her with a firm hand on her arm.

'Take no notice of sister. It is she who is the social climber. You should see her with senior officers!'

'It's kind of you, but perhaps others, too, see me as a social climber.'

'No, of course not. Kate's jealous of you because when we've gone and this house returns to normal, it will all be yours one day.'

'And she thinks I deliberately set out to ensnare Barney?'

Looking around the room and glimpsing villagers in the singing throng around the piano, she wondered how many of them thought the same. But this was so far from the truth that she smiled, but without humour. Seeing nothing beyond the upward lift of her mouth, William patted her shoulder.

'That's the spirit! She's not worth it. Damn what other people think. I just hope Barney realises how lucky . . .'

He got no farther, for the door was flung open behind them by Mrs Tabley who was making sure everyone noticed her entrance. After all, she was Lady of The Manor!

That evening, Christmas dinner at Dower Cottage was a quiet affair. Having assumed Hugo would dine with them, Mrs Tabley had not invited him formally. So when she went to leave the manor, she had beckoned him to come with her. She had made no attempt to hide her mortification when he told her that several days ago he had been invited to dine with the officers and senior nurses. Rose, too, was downcast for she had been looking forward to Hugo being at Dower Cottage.

Then Kate Clark came over, to gushingly wish Mrs Tabley a happy Christmas, but it was to Rose she darted a victorious smile. Then, linking her arm through Hugo's, Kate edged her voice with huskiness as she reminded him it was time they also thought of dining. Rose had become a quick learner and so, sweetly but quietly, voiced the hope that all the medical staff would enjoy the meal with no interruptions needed for emptying bedpans.

Sitting around the Dower Cottage dining table, the beauty of the centrepiece of holly and Christmas roses did little to cheer either Mrs Tabley or Rose, for after several hours spent with the wounded men they were both emotionally drained. The gaiety of those well enough to join in the festivities had an almost frenetic, hysterical quality, whilst in the quiet wards above, men lay in deep depression caused by either mental or physical wounds.

Both Mrs Tabley and Rose had spent time

there, trying to bring some comfort and Rose was surprised and touched by the tenderness Mrs Tabley showed. They were both thinking of Barney, Rose remembering the happy, carefree days when they were children, before the war had changed everything. Would Barney have wanted to marry her if there had been no war? She doubted it, for life would have continued as it had always done and so it would have been unthinkable for him to have taken a wife not of his own class.

Strangely, it was in the dimmer light of the candles on the table that Rose noticed how haggard Mrs Tabley looked, older, careworn. Leaning over to touch her hand, Rose reassured her softly.

'Barney will be all right, I know he will.'

'The young are always so optimistic,' was the sad reply.

Both retired early and it was only when she went to turn down the oil lamp that Rose saw the two parcels on her bed. For a second she frowned down at them, before remembering that both William and Hugo had brought her gifts. Dear Annie must have found William's and knowing her mistress would disapprove of such a gesture, the maid had taken it to Rose's room.

Sitting on her bed, William's was the first she opened and she smiled as she took out a small notebook bound in deep pink velvet. Used to the very practical life at the farm, such a gift seemed to have no purpose, except as a thing of beauty. Running a finger over the soft material, Rose knew she would never use it but would always treasure it.

It was several seconds before she broke the red sealing-wax on the string knots of Hugo's brown-paper-wrapped gift. By the shape, she knew it contained a book and wondered if it was one of his. It had only been days before that Mrs Tabley had complained to Hugo that she had been unable to buy any of his books. She then accused him of modesty in not giving her a copy himself. Hurriedly, he had changed the subject.

Now, carefully breaking the sealing-wax and undoing the string, Rose smoothed back the wrapping paper. But this did not reveal what she had expected, for the book was of Shakespearean love sonnets. With eyes suddenly brimming with tears, she opened it, looking for a personal inscription, but there was none. After all, how could there be, when she was promised to someone else?

The New Year, 1916, was two weeks old when Mrs Tabley received the news she had been praying would never happen. Barney had been wounded! The telegram had arrived whilst Rose was working at the farm and when she saw Seymour coming up the lane in the governess cart, she knew instantly it was bad news.

As she ran to open the farmyard gate,

Seymour gasped out, 'Miss Rose, come quickly! Madam's had a really bad turn. It's Mr Barney, he's been wounded.'

Madge ran out of the kitchen, Flora from her distilling room and it was she who snatched the bucket of potatoes Rose was carrying.

'I'll take those. Get your coat and go with Seymour. Mrs Tabley will need you. I pray to God Barney isn't badly injured.'

But Flora wasn't only thinking of Barney. If he had been badly injured, maimed, then she knew Rose would never leave him, even though it meant a loveless marriage, at least on her part.

On the journey to the cottage, despite the dread gripping her, Rose ordered Seymour to let the sweating horse go at an easier pace.

Asking Seymour if Mrs Tabley had been calmed with medicinal brandy, he replied anxiously that she was refusing everything, even a cup of sweet tea. Seeing Rose, Mrs Tabley flung wide her arms.

'Dear child, you must be in need of comfort, too.'

From behind her mistress, Annie held up the brandy glass, signalling to Rose the necessity of its contents being taken by Mrs Tabley. But shaking her head, Rose mouthed that Seymour should go for the doctor. Barney's distraught mother needed a far stronger sedative than brandy.

A call from the lady of the manor always brought immediate attention from the doctor and soon his patient was lying on her bed, drifting into a deep sleep. Rose, too, was offered a sedative, but refused. Mrs Tabley, when she came to, would need company, comforting, but also Rose's emotions were in such a terrible confusion that she needed both a clear head and time to try to disentangle them.

When Annie came into the drawing-room with a tray of light lunch, Rose turned from the window where she had been staring out at the garden as bleak now as her thoughts. Anxiously she asked about Mrs Tabley, her obvious distress having affected Rose deeply.

'Madam's sleeping peacefully. If you'll excuse me, I know it's not my place to be telling you what to do, but after you've tried to eat a little, you should get some fresh air. If madam comes round, I'll send Seymour for you, so you'd better tell me where you're going. If you don't mind me saying so, you would be best not going up to that hospital. It's no use upsetting yourself by seeing those poor lads and then imagining Mr Barney like them.'

When Rose murmured she would walk around the lake, Annie smiled sympathetically for she knew that as children Rose and Barney had often spent many happy hours there.

As she paced around the steel-grey, calm water, Rose would have been able to see

Hugo's cottage but she kept her eyes averted. Now was not the time to even glance in Hugo's direction. She had to concentrate on Barney. Was he well enough to think about her? If she thought and prayed hard enough, would he be able to sense it in some way? Slipping off the ribbon holding his ring, she held it tightly as though the warmth of her hand would help him.

As the tears prickling her eyes threatened to spill over, she tried to think more positively, optimistically. A duck rising in alarm from the lake made her look up. Hugo was running towards her.

'Rose, it is you? I saw someone shadowy here when I looked out of my window. What's wrong?' he called out.

She waited for him to reach her before telling him about Barney. Hugo made as though to take her hand, but when she shook her head, he let his arm drop limply by his side. He wanted to comfort her but realised she would consider any physical contact, however slight, would be disloyal to Barney at this time.

'Do you know the extent of his injuries, where he is?'

She shook her head then continued her slow, sad, thoughtful walk. But a fleeting smile indicated she would not be averse to his company.

'Do you think they'll send him to the

manor?' she asked suddenly.

'I don't know, perhaps they will.'

'His mother would like that.'

'And you? How would you feel seeing him wounded?'

Stopping, she turned to face him and, seeing the anguish in her eyes, he reacted with passion, putting his arms around her. For an instant she stiffened, but then with a sigh edged with tears, she relaxed against him.

'I don't want to imagine Barney hurt in any way. I've tried to prepare myself by thinking the worst, broken bones, wounds.'

'It is hard to think of those we love in any way but happy and well.'

'I've known him so long, all of my life. It's as though he's family.'

A chill swept over Hugo both physically and emotionally. If Rose saw Barney as being like part of the family, then joining his family would only seem a natural progression.

'I must go to the hospital, try to find out if they know anything or can find out something.'

Pulling away from him, she was running from the lake before he could do more than just whisper her name sadly.

Rose burst through the door of the manor in such obvious agitation that a nurse hurried towards her. Knowing of Rose's relationship to Barney Tabley, she guessed what had happened.

'He's not here. If he were, we would have

told you immediately.'

'Do you think they will send him here?'

'I don't know. They might, seeing this was his home, but it might not be for some time.'

William Dawson came hurrying down the stairs and at the sight of him, his resemblance to Barney made Rose burst into tears.

'Come on, let's go into the conservatory. There'll be no-one there. The doctors are doing their rounds.'

Guiding her to a wicker bench and sitting beside her, he took her hand.

'It's Barney, isn't it? He might not be badly injured.'

'It's the not knowing. William, could you try to find out?'

'I'll try but I don't hold out much hope.'

'Ah, there you are, William!'

Kate Clark suddenly flung open the conservatory doors as though hoping to find them in a compromising situation. The nurse who had first seen Rose had told the sister, thinking she would be better able to help the distressed girl than an officer. Kate had hurried to the conservatory, but her main concern was not to help Rose.

'William, I think the colonel is looking for you and you know how he hates to be kept waiting. Don't worry about Miss Edmunds. I'll send an orderly with some tea.'

Torn between his duty to a superior and to a girl he admired greatly, William hesitated.

90

Frowning anxiously he asked Rose if she would be all right and as she nodded he promised to do all he could to find out about Barney.

'There's no need for tea, thank you,' Rose said with cold politeness as she crossed to the door.

She wanted to say something pithy which would wipe the half-smile from Kate's face but her thoughts were too preoccupied with Barney. So, head held high, she left, Kate slamming the conservatory door with such force that the glass rattled ominously.

William Dawson did his best to discover any information about Barney, but with countless wounded flooding back, records were chaotic. Rose was torn between going back to work at the farm and staying with Mrs Tabley who, although still distraught, was refusing to take the doctor's sedative. Although Rose hinted that with so many men away in the army, the farm was short-handed and she was really needed, Mrs Tabley refused to let her return, even for a couple of hours a day.

When Mrs Tabley said she was going to lie down, Rose seized a rare opportunity to go into the kitchen where Cook plied her with strong tea and freshly-baked ginger biscuits. She was unaware that Flora had called to express her concern. After Annie had enquired of her mistress if she would receive the visitor, Flora was shown to Mrs Tabley's bedroom where for once she was greeted warmly. A woman of her own class, or very nearly, would understand the delicate state of her nerves, and Flora did, for she brought calming, soothing, herbal preparations.

Rose knew nothing of this until Annie returned to the kitchen.

'Mother here, with Mrs Tabley?' she said in astonishment.

Rose hurriedly got to her feet, nearly spilling her tea in the process.

'Now then, there's no need to fret. Your mother is tending madam, who's thoroughly enjoying the lavender balms and lotions. You stay put. You've danced enough attendance on madam as it is.'

But even though she did stay in the kitchen, Rose listened for any sounds of discord from above. Her mother could be tactless and Mrs Tabley was always easily upset, never more so than now. She was relieved when Flora came in to say that her patient was sleeping like a baby and to instruct Annie in giving her calming cowslip cordial.

'And you, my dear, how are you?' Flora asked, turning to Rose.

Although she appeared to be busy instructing Annie, Flora had been observing her daughter.

'I've no need for any of your concoctions,' was the sharp reply, and, meeting her mother's searching gaze, Rose hoped none of her inner turmoil was visible.

'No, I can see that,' Flora replied quietly.

Skilled though she was, she had no remedy for her daughter's troubled spirit. Although Flora believed every problem would come to a natural resolution given time, now she wished with all her heart that the natural resolution of Rose's promise to Barney would not be marriage. She left deep in thought, pausing where the grassy path divided into two, one going to Good Pasture, the other to Hugo's cottage. Her mind was suddenly made up and she went towards the cottage.

* * *

Although after much heart-searching, Hugo did indeed act on Flora's advice, he did not call at Dower Cottage until two days later. He wanted to express his concern to Mrs Tabley but at the same time backed away from doing so. Rose would be there and after Flora's visit he had spent hours thinking about what she had said. Although for once she had not spoken directly, preferring Hugo to make his own deductions, Flora had made it plain that Rose was deeply unhappy, but she did not say exactly why.

After reluctantly burying his own secret hopes, he reasoned any right-thinking girl would be unhappy in the circumstances, not knowing if a sweetheart was badly injured.

An unheard action by Mrs Tabley began his

visit, for before he could lift the brass lion-head door knocker, she had opened the door.

'Mrs Tabley, I . . .'

He trailed off, then was even more amazed when she smiled.

'Rose does her best to distract me, but I keep looking out for a telegram, a letter or perhaps someone from the manor with news, but do come in. I'm sure Rose will welcome seeing a younger face.'

Hearing voices in the hall, Seymour appeared, only to be waved away by Mrs Tabley ordering him to find Rose and see that coffee was brought to the drawing-room. Reluctantly, Rose went to the drawing-room, pausing outside the door to straighten her shoulders and fix an expression on her face which she hoped would show polite thanks for Hugo's visit.

'Come along, Miss Rose, it's no use standing there like a statue.'

Annie had come bustling up with a laden tray.

'It would be a kindness if you opened the door for me. Where would you like me to put the tray for you to pour?'

'Oh, anywhere will do,' was the snapped reply.

'Isn't dear Rose a brave girl?' Mrs Tabley demanded of Hugo as Rose poured. 'Such self-control in such terrible circumstances. I have high hopes of her as dear Barney's wife.'

Lips compressed, cheeks reddening, Rose crashed down the coffee pot with a force which had Mrs Tabley shaking a reproving finger at her. This was so like a teacher reprimanding a naughty child and fearing Rose would react hastily, Hugo hurriedly offered to play the piano.

'Something soothing,' Mrs Tabley ordered, settling back in her chair.

'Miss Edmunds, perhaps you would turn the pages,' Hugo asked, crossing to the grand piano.

Even though Rose had done this many times before when he demonstrated something during her lessons or played for Mrs Tabley, she hesitated. Then as Hugo turned to her with a questioning lift of an eyebrow, she went towards the piano. But, she told herself, she would not allow herself to forget Barney for one second. He needed her, wherever he was.

She had always felt Hugo was very perceptive of the mood of others, knowing the time for light-hearted conversation and a time to be silent, so she was not surprised when he seemed totally preoccupied with the music, a small nod indicating when a page needed turning. He played for nearly twenty minutes only occasionally pausing to check that Mrs Tabley wished him to continue which she indicated with a wave of her hand. But when it was obvious she had fallen asleep, he stood up, miming that he would leave.

Rose followed him into the hall and as she began to thank him politely for playing, he took a piece of music from his overall pocket.

'I would like you to look at this before your next lesson,' he said. 'But as Mrs Tabley won't wish to be disturbed and you are doing so well reading music, I suggest you look at it in your room.'

Rose frowned. What a strange suggestion. But then as she took the music, she felt an extra thickness between the leaves. When she looked up at him with questioning eyes, what she saw in his had her hurrying to her room.

CHAPTER SEVEN

There was no key in the lock on Rose's bedroom door so to prevent any intrusion, she leaned against it whilst reading the two pages torn from a small notebook. In a firm clear hand, Hugo had written his message.

Dear Rose,
I know I don't have the right to address you so in the meaning I fully intend, but this will be for the first and last time. Although we have behaved properly, though at times perhaps a little foolishly, considering your position, I feel that you, too, feel that had things been different, there might have been a future for us together. But

even as I write this, I know certain facts which you do not, which might still have tipped the scales against us.

Those for whom I work have ordered me to move on in a few days' time and in the circumstances, I know it would be for the best for both of us. Whatever has happened to Barney, I pray it's not serious. He will need you now more than ever before. When the time comes, you will make a most excellent Lady of the Manor, kind, perceptive and very caring for all those on the estate.

It would be wrong of me to write what is in my heart but I shall always remember you with the deepest affection. Be as happy as you can.

Hugo.

Rose did not have to re-read the letter, for every word was seared into her memory. But what did he mean by those for whom he worked? She knew nothing about writing books, but surely authors did not work for someone who could order where they lived? She was so deep in thought that she was totally unaware of the sudden commotion in the house until Annie came running up the stairs calling her name.

'Miss Rose! It's Mr Barney! They've sent word from the manor. He's not badly injured, got all his limbs and such. He's asking for you.'

For a few seconds Rose stood as though turned to stone but then Annie pushed open the door and this brought Rose to life.

'When did he arrive?' she asked, hurrying to the wardrobe for her coat. 'Does Mrs Tabley know?'

'Madam ran out of the house just as she was, as soon as she knew. Seymour's gone after her with a coat.'

As Rose passed Annie in the doorway, the maid put a hand on her arm.

'Miss Rose, I know I'm speaking as I shouldn't but you go steady when you see Mr Barney. Don't go saying anything you might regret later. There'll be plenty of time to talk about personal matters.'

Frowning, Rose touched the hidden signet ring.

'And,' Annie continued softly, 'you had better come up with a good reason for hiding that and all. But before you put it on show, you just think what that will mean. I've known you since you were a small child and I wouldn't want you to be doing anything foolish.'

Rose's reply was a brief nod, but from her slight smile, Annie knew she had not taken offence. She watched as Rose hurried downstairs, buttoning her coat against the chill east wind. Then from the landing window, the anxious maid saw her walking quickly towards the manor. What Annie did not see was that out of sight of both houses, Rose stopped. Recalling Annie's words, she wondered what she had meant. Was it a warning about Barney

98

and their relationship? Had the maid guessed about Hugo?

Although the manor had been his home, Barney was in the drawing-room ward along with other wounded. Sister Kate Clark was fussing around him, plumping pillows, reassuring Mrs Tabley and ordering a nurse to bring tea.

'Barney! How are you?' Rose asked anxiously from the foot of the bed.

'How would you expect him to feel seeing he's in a hospital bed?' the sister said so acidly that even Mrs Tabley looked up in astonishment.

'I'm all the better for seeing you,' Barney answered and smiled. 'Come here and hold my hand.'

As Kate Clark showed no sign of moving, Rose knew instinctively that the sister was trying to exclude her.

'If those pillows need any more attention, Mrs Tabley and I will be able to manage,' Rose said firmly. 'I'm sure you have more than enough to do.'

Glancing at her patient and seeing the way his gaze was fixed on Rose, his hand outstretched, Sister Clark left. But as she turned away, Rose was puzzled to see a look of . . . was it cunning?

Barney's unexpectedly tight grasp on her hand had Rose holding her breath to prevent a gasp from escaping. He was still looking at her, but in a way which made her drop her gaze to their clasped hands. It was as though he was trying to read not only her thoughts, but what had happened to her since he had left. But she was saved from talking by Mrs Tabley's non-stop chatter. Then abruptly Barney lost his patience, ordering his mother to be quiet and in such harsh tones that tears trickled down her cheeks.

'Sorry, Mother,' he said. 'I've been through a lot.'

'You poor lamb,' Mrs Tabley began, but Rose interrupted quietly with the suggestion that they came back later when Barney had rested.

As they walked away, Rose glanced back at Barney, pity welling tears in her eyes. Lying against the white pillows, face ashen, unshaven, his eyes appeared even more sunken because of the prominence of the bones above the hollows of his cheeks. She understood more clearly than if he had spoken something of what he had seen, endured. But she had not long to dwell on this for once out in the hall, Mrs Tabley was demanding to see the most senior doctor and in such a loud voice that Rose hurriedly tried to silence her.

'Don't you go hushing me! This is my house, my son and I demand . . .'

'Mrs Tabley, do come into my office. You've had quite a shock.'

Sister Clark's sympathy immediately

soothed Barney's mother, but Rose detected a note of insincerity. With a smile of satisfaction that her status had been recognised, Mrs Tabley allowed herself to be guided to the small office which had once held the garden furniture.

'There's not much space,' Kate Clark threw over her shoulder at Rose. 'Only room for two, but Mrs Tabley is the captain's mother.'

As the door was closed almost in her face, Rose frowned at the news that Barney was now a captain. Since when? He hadn't mentioned it in his last few letters which admittedly had become briefer, more disjointed as he and his men moved into the firing line. Not wanting to appear to be listening at the door, Rose moved away, but then stopped uncertainly. Should she look in on Barney again? Should she wait for Mrs Tabley? But she decided against the latter for she did not want to see Kate Clark again, perhaps be subjected to a comment so cleverly disguised that only Rose would be aware of its barbs.

'Rose, you look dreadful!'

William Dawson was coming towards her, then as he realised the crassness of his remark, he stammered an apology before adding, 'Barney isn't really hurt all that badly, not compared with some. He's been hit in the legs by shrapnel. He shouldn't be here by rights. We don't usually take cases like his until they are more on the road to recovery but when I

101

chanced on his name as a casualty . . .'

'Thank you,' Rose said quietly. 'It will mean a lot to his mother to have him here.'

That she did not include herself made William wonder if he had acted wisely, for it was for Rose's sake that he had pulled strings. But before either of them could say anything more, the colonel was shouting for him.

'Sorry, Rose, must leave you. Go home, have a rest, collect your thoughts.'

'I'd better wait for Mrs Tabley.'

'Oh, for goodness' sake, Dower Cottage is little more than a stone's throw away!' William exclaimed with unaccustomed impatience.

Nevertheless, it was with a feeling of guilt that Rose left, but she had not long to wonder if she had done the right thing, for Hugo came hurrying along the path towards her.

'Barney, is he all right? I've only just heard.'

'Yes. They say he isn't seriously injured.'

With words of Hugo's letter springing vividly into her thoughts, her reply was a monotone. She hadn't had time to think, to consider the full import of his letter. She continued on her way and after the briefest of hesitations, he fell in step beside her.

'Rose, my letter, have you read it?'

Nodding, she increased her speed and, taking this as an indication that she did not want his company, he stopped. He watched her, cursing silently that he had given in to such a whim. But what he felt for her was no whim.

Although Mrs Tabley spent most of the following days with Barney, at times it seemed to Rose that she resented her being there, too, even though her visits were short because of the farm work. Mrs Tabley had been very annoyed when Rose had decided to go back to work. Mrs Tabley had hoped Rose would not want to resume her previous life. When she pleaded with Barney to make Rose see sense, he replied shortly that he didn't own Rose, she could do what she liked. But his mother's continual trivial chatter and fussing drove him so much to distraction that he confided in Kate Clark, begging her to find some excuse so he could have some peace.

As Rose went into Dower Cottage kitchen after work, seeing glum faces, her first thought was that Barney had taken a turn for the worse, but Annie's swift explanation had her sighing wearily.

'It's madam. She's been told not to spend so much time with Mr Barney. He needs rest and no doubt so do the rest of them in that ward!' Annie added with a wry smile. 'Madam says you've to go into the drawing-room as soon as you got in, never mind changing out of your working clothes.'

'She must be in a state then,' Rose muttered as she headed off.

'Sit down,' Mrs Tabley ordered. 'I'm sure they're keeping something from me,' she went on, a catch in her voice. 'When that sister said I must curtail my visits for the sake of Barney's health, I demanded to see a doctor but was told they were all too busy. Busy drinking tea and flirting with the nurses, more like! Barney needs me, his mother! Didn't I nurse him through measles, mumps and whooping cough?'

When Mrs Tabley continued venting her outrage, Rose hurriedly intervened with an offer to try to find out if indeed there was anything seriously wrong with Barney. She would do so the following morning, on her way to the farm.

'You can't go to a hospital in working clothes! Whatever will they think?'

'I won't be going into a ward.'

The following morning, Rose did not go to the manor in her working clothes, not because of Mrs Tabley, but she did not want to give Sister Clark the opportunity for another sly remark.

Going into the entrance hall and seeing orderlies hurrying about with washing bowls and towels, she was suddenly aware that perhaps she should not have come. She was just on the point of leaving when the ward door was thrust open by a wheel-chair.

'Rose, I couldn't believe it when an orderly said you were here,' Barney said irritably. 'If it's Mother having one of her turns, I don't want to know.'

'Sorry, I shouldn't have come so early,' she flustered.

'Well, now you are here, you'd better tell me what's wrong. Push me over there by that bench. I haven't got the hang of this chair yet.'

Awkward with embarrassment, Rose found the wheel-chair difficult to manoeuvre, her ineptitude making Barney swear harshly.

'Sorry,' she murmured, perching on the edge of the bench.

'Stop saying sorry and get on with what you want to say and it had better be important.'

'Your mother is upset because she's been told she mustn't visit so often. She's worried doctors are keeping something from her.'

'Too right they are! But seeing this is her house, no-one wants to offend her, but if she was here right now, I'd tell her straight.'

Rose went to take his hand to calm him, but he snatched it away.

'I'd tell her I'm sick of her fussing about, always here, treating me like I'm a piece of her wretched, precious porcelain. I'm not badly wounded, I've all my limbs and senses. It would be an eye opener to you both to see what I've seen.'

Swallowing back another apology, Rose looked down at her tight-clenched hands.

'I know we can't possibly imagine what it's like, but that's what makes it so difficult for people like your mother and me. We want to help but don't know how.'

'It's a different world over there.'

Barney's faced was etched with deep lines of remembering.

'You can never understand what it's like.'

'I could try.'

'I doubt it. Anyway, what do you know of life, other than what goes on in the farm and village? You're stuck in a muddy rut which has absolutely nothing to do with the real world.'

'Barney, I know you must have changed but I can't help it if I haven't. That doesn't mean that I can't help.'

'Help? In what way? You and mother are both happy in your cosy, little worlds. Neither of you has the slightest idea of what this damn war is.'

'That's not our fault,' Rose replied looking at him directly.

As their eyes met, she shivered. His were as hard as stone, cold, shuttered in an odd, frightening way, but before either of them could speak, Sister Clark's commanding voice shouted out at Rose.

'What do you think you're doing?'

As she strode across the hall, Barney soothed, 'It's all right, Kate. She doesn't know hospital routine. She's going. The cows need their milkmaid!'

'She has no right to be here, upsetting you.'

'She is just going,' Rose said icily and getting up she walked towards the door, half expecting Barney to say something, call a

106

goodbye, but when he did not, she half turned. Kate Clark was bending over him, smoothing back his hair. He was smiling, not just the polite mouth-movement of thanks, but how he had once smiled at her.

CHAPTER EIGHT

After hurrying back to Dower Cottage to reassure Mrs Tabley that the truth about Barney's condition was not being kept from her, Rose changed into her working clothes. She was just lacing her boots at the back door when Annie crossed the yard from the apple store.

'Apple dumplings tonight then?' Rose asked.

'Yes!' was the abrupt reply. Then, 'Miss Rose, have you a minute? There's something I think you should know, but I don't want to talk here.'

As Rose nodded, Annie shouted to Cook that some of the apples were rotten and she was going back to the store. Taking the hint, Rose followed. Once inside the apple-scented shed, Rose sighed.

'Which of Mrs Tabley's numerous deadly sins have I committed now?'

'It's not what you've done, it's what she's up to, there,' Annie rushed out, jerking a work-

107

roughened thumb towards the manor.

Because of what had happened so recently, Rose assumed Annie was referring to Mrs Tabley's visits to Barney, so she was taken aback when the maid launched into a tirade against Sister Kate Clark.

'I've heard from my brother's youngest girl who helps up there that there's gossip a-plenty about that stuck-up Sister Clark. Seems she toadies to the doctors and officers enough to make you sick, and she tries to order about servants who are nothing to do with her.'

'I'm sorry, but I don't see what this has to do with me.'

Rose was halfway through the door when Annie's next pronouncement stopped her.

'She's after Mr Barney!'

'Sister Clark after Barney? What on earth do you mean? Anyway, gossip is the favourite pastime around here.'

'I don't gossip!'

Annie's denial was so injured, Rose quickly apologised. Then suddenly remembering the cameo of a scene she had glimpsed that very morning as she left the manor, she asked quietly, 'Exactly what have you heard?'

'She spends more time than she should with Mr Barney.'

'Perhaps he needs a little more nursing attention.'

'My brother's girl sometimes takes the tea round the wards and she's heard that sister talking to Mr Barney about the house and estate, questioning him, saying how lovely it all is.'

Rose left, muttering something about the incident being no more than a nurse just taking an interest in a patient.

'You never were one for seeing the bad in anyone!' Annie called out after her. Then more cheerfully she added, 'But you never know, things have a way of turning out for the best.'

Reaching the farm much later than usual, Rose was just passing her mother's distilling room when she stopped in amazement. She had never known her father set foot inside, but now, although the door was closed, she could hear his deep voice. Assuming her parents were having a private discussion or more likely, a disagreement, she began to move away when she heard Hugo's name.

'Edward, how many times do I have to tell you? They mean to harm Hugo and if you're willing to stand by and let it happen, I am not!'

Flora came out so suddenly that Rose had no time to move away.

'And where have you been?' Flora demanded. 'I never thought you would be one to take to rising late like lie-a-bed Mrs Tabley. There's work to be done here. Your father can't manage.'

'Flora, be quiet!'

It was so unusual for Edward to raise his

voice that both Flora and Rose looked at him in astonishment. Then he seemed to reach a decision.

'Rose, I could do with a hand rounding up the ewes in Lower Meadow. I want them nearer the house where the dogs can keep those foxes away.'

'But they're not due to lamb for a few weeks yet,' Rose said, puzzled.

'We're moving them now,' Edward repeated firmly, then turning to Flora he ordered, 'And you can get back to your herbs. Leave this to me.'

Taking the dogs with them, Rose and her father walked to the field in a deep silence. Reaching Lower Meadow gate, Edward leaned on it, staring unseeingly at the sheep, oblivious of Rose's anxious frown, of the eager dogs at his feet. Although he was always a quiet man, slow to show any emotion, there was a hard set to his jaw, a weary sadness in his eyes. Rose threaded her arm through his, then rested her head on his shoulder.

'I heard Hugo's name mentioned,' she said.

'War is such a terrible thing. It's bad enough when it kills or maims, but when it turns unreasonable, law-abiding men into unheeding, vengefulness . . .'

She saw his eyes drift across the fields, looking towards the lake.

'This has got something to do with Hugo, hasn't it? What is it? Are you going to tell me, or am I going to have to ask Mother?'

'They think he's a German spy,' Edward replied flatly.

'A spy?' she repeated incredulously. 'I suppose this is drink talking. Some people never do take kindly to strangers, even though Hugo's been here for months.'

'It's his name. When he was sorting the letters at the post office, Saul's attention was caught by Spanish stamps on the envelope that had been readdressed from London. Then he saw the name, Schmidt. The address was Hugo's. Saul showed it to one of the boys back from France who said Schmidt was the German for Smith.'

'But Hugo's as English as we are! He doesn't have an accent, and I know he went to school in Worcester, which is why he came here to write. He remembered the area. And what's more, he doesn't even look German!'

Edward was finding this turn of events hard to take in, without Rose's naïve comments.

'And what does a German look like?' he said angrily. 'Aren't they ordinary folk who look like us, two arms, two legs, two eyes?'

'But what about Hugo? What happened? He's not in any danger, is he?'

'He's gone on one of his trips to London, so he's safe for the time being. Rose, you don't know where he goes, do you? An address?'

As she shook her head, they faced each other with identical anxiety.

111

'A couple of the lads, exempt from the army because of their jobs, don't want to pass up the chance of being heroes. They came marching up to the farm this morning, demanding to know what I knew about Hugo. I told them that as far as I was concerned he was a good customer who paid regularly.'

'They didn't hurt you, did they?'

'They didn't get the chance! Your mother set the dogs on them!'

Edward smiled briefly at the remembrance of the men running away, threatening to turn him in to the police for befriending a spy.

'What are we going to do?' Rose appealed to her father.

'I told them he'd ordered milk for the day after tomorrow.'

'Dad, how could you?'

'Quite easily. It isn't true. Hugo told me he would call for milk tomorrow.'

'So there's time to warn him then,' Rose asked anxiously.

'They'll be watching the cottage.'

'Not now they won't! After Mrs Tabley has gone to bed, I'll drop a note into Hugo's cottage,' Rose insisted.

'No, I absolutely forbid you to get involved!'

'You've involved me already, Father,' Rose replied, a cheeky smile dimpling her cheek. 'Look, Dad, if there is anyone about tonight, I've spent long enough around the lake when Barney and I were children to see without being seen.'

Although Hugo was uppermost in their minds, nothing more was said about him, except when they returned to the farm, Edward reassured Flora that he had the matter in hand. When she began to demand to know what he intended doing, he told her to be quiet, they could trust no-one. To the surprise of Edward and Rose, Flora came to work with them, something she never did, but they said nothing, knowing in times of great anxiety, it was good to be with others.

It was only when Rose was leaving the dairy after the last milking of the day that Edward slipped her a note addressed to Hugo.

'You will take care, won't you?' he urged.

'I'll be fine, don't worry.'

Rose was crossing the farmyard when Flora's quiet call from the distilling room made her retrace her steps.

'Rose, your father isn't the only one to have made plans,' Flora whispered with an edge of smugness. 'If Hugo needs somewhere to hide, to think, he can use this place. No-one dares to come here and if those village louts do try, I'll threaten to drench them with a vile liquid.'

'You wouldn't, would you?' Rose questioned.

'Of course not! But a wetting with lavender water would certainly make their lives unbearable with the other men!'

Rose laughed, then set off for Dower

Cottage.

Going into Dower Cottage's kitchen, Rose did not have to be told that Mrs Tabley had been issuing non-stop orders, demanding instant attention.

'She's going on and on about Mr Barney,' Annie said, filling a large copper jug with hot water for Rose. 'She's taken to her bed, says worry is exhausting her. She's been rambling on about a mother's love being the most precious but painful bond. Cook thinks she's losing her senses. Although Seymour has been up to the manor with notes for the doctor and Mr Barney, he's always been intercepted by that sister I warned you about. All she says is Mr Barney needs peace and quiet. You should have seen madam's face when she heard that! Miss Rose, I know you were up at the manor this morning, but if any of us is to have a good night's sleep . . .'

'All right, I'll go, but I'd better see Mrs Tabley first.'

'There's no need. Madam is sleeping like a baby,' Annie said. 'You go and see Mr Barney and we'll have a nice meal waiting for you. Then by the look of you, it will be an early bed.'

Although Anne's remark about an early bed would give Rose the ideal excuse for going to her room in the hope the servants would do the same, she was annoyed and upset that she had to go to the manor and possibly face Sister

Clark again. Besides, Barney was safe, Hugo was not and it was he who was the centre of her constant worry. She should be trying to help him, not running after Mrs Tabley and her foolish notions.

Rose took a muddy short-cut to the manor, eager to be as quick as possible. But Flora would have said it was fate which took Rose past the dimly-lit conservatory. It was Kate Clark's voice which brought her thoughts sharply back from Hugo. Pausing, she heard a man's low voice followed by Kate Clark's flirtatious laugh. Keeping to the concealment of some laurels, Rose hurried on. If Kate was with someone in the conservatory, then she would be able to slip into Barney's ward. She was just crossing the hall when a young girl, carrying a tray of water glasses, hurried towards her.

'Miss, you don't know me, but Annie's my aunt.'

Rose smiled vaguely.

'If you're after seeing Mr Tabley, he's in the conservatory,' she gabbled.

Then as though regretting what she had said, she hurried away. Rose stood still, then a violent shiver coursed through her. She went slowly towards the source of the laughter she had heard. It was as though she was in a dream, moving without actually putting one foot in front of the other. Opening the conservatory door slowly, she stood silhouetted against the bright light from the hall.

'Oh, no! It's Rose!' Barney exploded.

She began a swift apology but as her eyes became accustomed to the dim light, she saw Barney push Kate Clark away. The sister had been bending over him and caught by the strength of his action, she staggered back, but this in no way hampered her tongue.

'Look, Barney, yet another servant from your doting mother. Oh, I'm sorry, it's not one of the indoor servants but the farm girl.'

'Kate, that's enough!' Barney ordered.

Then holding out his hand to Rose, his apology tumbled out.

'Rose, has that awful mother of mine sent you to check on me yet again? Really, you shouldn't let her have you running about like this.'

'She's worried.'

Her hand on Barney's shoulder, Kate Clark snapped, 'There's nothing for her to worry about as I've already told her. She might own this place, but we have more important things to be doing than dealing with her fancies.'

'Yes, I'm sure you have, so I'll not keep you,' Rose said evenly. 'But before you go, do straighten your cap.'

Watching Kate Clark leave, Barney muttered to Rose, 'I'm sorry.'

'Sorry for what?' she asked evenly, turning up the oil lamp on the table.

116

'Don't do that!'

Hastily he shielded his eyes, but not before she caught a glimpse of an expression which took her back to the boy-Barney caught in mischief, or only last autumn, the man-Barney caught by Hugo in the cornfield.

'What exactly was Sister Clark doing here? Shouldn't you be in the ward and in bed?'

'You sound just like Mother,' he blustered. 'For goodness' sake, you're not my nanny!'

'No, I'm your . . .'

She stopped, frowning, her hand going to his signet ring against the skin of her throat. What exactly was she to Barney? Although he had asked her to marry him, there had been no formal engagement, no announcement.

'Barney, exactly what am I to you?' she demanded. 'You and that sister seem very friendly.'

'I do believe you're jealous!'

She stood in front of him and although she appeared to be looking down at him, what she was seeing were flashbacks of scenes—him, almost tearfully, making her promise to wait for him . . . his signet ring. It all seemed so unreal, as though it was not her who had been involved. Her silence and sightless stare unnerved Barney into hasty excuses.

'Kate and I often talk. She's interested in this house, the estate. Her family has a similar place in Gloucestershire so she feels at home here.'

'Does she indeed!'

There was no irony in Rose's remark, only amusement.

'I expect you both know the same people, the county set.'

'What if we do? It's good to talk about something other than the war. She realises I need to forget.'

'And I don't? I might not have been there, but I read the papers, talk to men who have come back.'

'Yes, but hang it all, Rose, you're just a girl.'

She knew he wasn't comparing her to men, but to Kate Clark.

'She's older than you,' she heard herself accuse.

'Not all that much, but anyway, why should that stop us talking? There's no law against it, is there? Questions, questions! You've been with my mother so long, you're beginning to sound like her!'

'Let me remind you, I didn't choose to live with her.'

'Oh, shut up! Leave me alone. What do you know about except cows and running errands?'

Without another word or a backward glance, Rose left.

By the time Rose had returned to Dower Cottage, Mrs Tabley was awake. This time she really did seem to be reassured when Rose told her Barney was fine.

'That's wonderful,' Mrs Tabley murmured,

118

closing her eyes and sinking back against a pile of lace-edged pillows. 'Having my boy back home, fit and well, is all I want, and of course you will be glad, too.'

Will I, Rose wondered, as she went to try to eat the meal Annie had waiting. Did she really want Barney back? He had left little more than a boy but inevitably war had changed him into a man. She rubbed her forehead. She couldn't think about Barney now, he could wait. Hugo was in trouble and she must not fail him.

The grandmother clock had just struck midnight when Rose finally decided everyone was asleep. For what she knew would be the last time, she took off the chain with Barney's signet ring, dropping them on to the dressing table. Then she dressed in dark clothes, a long scarf wound around her head and partially obscuring her face, and slipped out of the back door, heading for the lake and Hugo's cottage.

Rose was just thrusting her father's note under Hugo's cottage door when she was seized from behind. When she cried out in alarm, she was twisted around to face her captor. They spoke the other's name in relieved unison but when they began to speak again at the same time, Hugo bade her be silent as, opening the door, he half-carried her inside.

'Rose, what are you doing here at this time of night?'

'I've come to warn you. Some of the village

men are after you. They think you're a spy!'

'I won't light a lamp or fire just in case someone comes snooping. We'll go upstairs so we won't be overheard.'

Taking her hand, he guided her up the twisting stairs to the only bedroom. Then with a wry smile which she could not see, he led her over to the bed. Just sitting there with Rose was not what his instincts wanted to do! But even had there not been pressing problems, he would have tried to suppress his desires out of respect for her. Tentatively, he put an arm around her and after the briefest of hesitations she leaned against him. He knew she was looking up at him for he could feel the warmth of her breath on his cheek.

'I knew something was up,' he whispered, dragging himself back reluctantly to the obvious troubles. 'Something made me approach the cottage cautiously, so when I saw a couple of men prowling about, trying the door and windows, I knew they were on to me.'

As Rose stiffened, he tightened his hold.

'Rose, it isn't what you think. I'm not a German spy. I work for British Intelligence. My knowledge of German and Germany is useful to them. You see, 'way back, over thirty years ago, long before any of this madness, my father was on the staff of the German Embassy in London. He met my mother at some function, they fell in love and married. When he was recalled to Germany, my mother went, too. I was just a baby and until I was sent here to boarding school, I spent a lot of time with my father's family. Can you imagine what I felt when war was declared? My father's country was fighting against my mother's. Even now, my relatives might be killing each other.'

'That's dreadful!' Rose sympathised, but did not allow herself to relax back against him. 'But why did you decide to work for us, not Germany?'

'I knew Germany, or rather the Kaiser and his advisors, were totally wrong. But believe me, the authorities here took some persuading that my motives were genuine! But eventually they let me translate documents, letters, advise them.'

'But why come here? Why not stay in London?'

'Before the war, I lived in London, writing for both German and English newspapers and so my new employers thought it best if I disappeared. Now they want me back in London and it looks just in time, from what I saw earlier. I know what I've told you might seem a total fabrication, but, Rose, I am speaking the truth.'

Feeling her nod, his murmured thanks was heartfelt. Then with a vehemence which startled her, he ground out, 'Damn this war! If things had been normal, peaceful, there is so much I would want to say to you, about how I feel.'

121

Happiness sweeping aside her fears, she laughed.

'If it wasn't for this war, we wouldn't have met. My mother would say it was fate.'

'And do you believe in fate? Or is it your fate to marry Barnaby?'

'Why do you sometimes call him Barnaby?'

'Oh, I don't know. Yes, I do! I fell in love with you the first time I came for milk, but seeing how you and he were always together, I wanted to keep him separate from you in my mind, so I used his full name.'

'But we weren't always together! Much of the time I was working on the farm.'

'When you weren't, you often seemed to be with him. Then there was that incident in the cornfield, then you moved in with his mother.'

'None of it was my doing, you know that.'

'I know, but you went along with it which must mean you feel something for him.'

'I do, but not . . .'

Suddenly shy, a little fearful, she stopped.

'But not as a woman should feel for a man?' Hugo prompted.

'Barney seemed so desperate for me to say I'd be here for him.'

'But even then you realised you didn't love him, other than perhaps as a childhood friend?' he asked urgently.

'I didn't look beyond the end of the war. No-one does.'

'And what about now? Are you looking

now? Rose, it might be a long time before we see each other again. Now it's my turn to ask you to wait for me. Will you, even though it might mean unpleasantness with Barnaby and his mother, your parents, even the villagers?'

'My life has been organised too much by other people. It's time I took charge of it.'

'So you will wait?'

'I'll wait, but I'll be counting.'

Not needing to hear more, he kissed her and her willing, eager response had them both forgetting the problems which lay ahead. It was the sudden, frantic barking of a dog which broke them apart.

'Rose, how selfish of me. Go now!'

'That was our dog barking at a fox,' she soothed. 'But I'm not leaving you until I know you're safe. It's you who should go.'

'I've only a few clothes but there are books and papers. They're of no value to anyone but I guess the men out to get me will destroy anything in their frustration at having missed me.'

'I'll help you pack,' Rose said with a briskness she was not feeling.

Although Hugo had to get away quickly, she would savour these last few minutes, try to remember every second.

'We'll close all the curtains and keep the lamp just high enough to see. I doubt anyone will be back until daybreak.'

They worked quickly, using the kitchen

table as a collection point. When their hands touched or their eyes met, they both had to force themselves to continue.

'There's too much here for you to carry by yourself,' she said finally. 'I think the best thing for you to do is to hide in Mother's distilling room as she suggested.'

'If I'm found there, it will mean trouble for your parents,' he said uncertainly.

'No-one would dare go in there! Some villagers think Mother is a witch!'

CHAPTER NINE

At the usual time, Rose walked into the farm kitchen. One look at her face told Flora that Hugo was in the distilling room but her only acknowledgement of this was a slight smile, a nod. Although she pressed Rose to eat, she refused, hurrying out to help her father with the milking. Sitting on a three-legged stool, her head against the comforting flank of her favourite cow, she forced herself to concentrate on the steady rhythm of her hands, the steady squirting of milk into the pail.

'You got him here then,' Edward said quietly as he wiped down the next cow. 'It's all right, I know. Your mother can't keep a secret!'

'We'd better move Hugo quickly then,' she said, worried.

'Although those men will hang about at the cottage for a while, it would be wisest for him to leave here as soon as possible.'

Then seeing her begin to rise, Edward pushed her back with a quiet reminder that the cows were in urgent need of milking and anyway, everything had to appear normal. But later, having quickly finished her work in the dairy, Rose managed to evade her father and slip into the distilling room.

'Hugo!' she whispered urgently into the herb-scented gloom.

The heavy, oppressive silence told her he had gone. Heart-stopping disappointment turning her legs to jelly, she fumbled for a chair. When had he left? Where had he gone? Why hadn't he said goodbye to her? Juddering sobs punctuated wild, disjointed thoughts. To have left like that must mean he really didn't love her. In similar circumstances she would never have left without seeing him! Then, remembering her father had deliberately kept her busy, away from the distilling room, she cried in anguish. Others had won yet again, organising her life.

When the door opened, Rose turned, furious, accusing words spilling in an uncontrollable torrent.

'Rose, dear child, we did it for the best,' Edward tried to soothe. 'It's best you weren't involved.'

'But I am involved! Don't you understand, any of you? I love him!'

'Your mother was right then,' Edward sighed.

Then, gently putting an arm around her shoulder, he held out a page torn from Flora's notebook of herbal remedies. Lighting the lamp, he left.

Dearest Rose, she read.

I've not much time. Flora has just told me it's time to leave. She's going on one of her herbal forages and I'm to shadow her at a distance. She won't tell me where we're going, for fear I'll tell you. But much as I love you, want you with me, I would never put you in danger. My love, I must go in body, but my heart remains here.

Bitter despair swamped her but this was swiftly dispelled by anger. How dare her parents leave her out of planning Hugo's escape! It was she who should be taking him, not Flora. They were treating her like a child again. No doubt they wanted Hugo out of the way, and wanted her to marry Barney. Getting up with a violence which sent the chair crashing on to the stone-flagged floor, she muttered, 'I'll show them all. It's my life!'

Stopping only to grab her coat, she ran from the farm, across to Dower Cottage. Seeing her go, Edward's expression was sorrowful.

Something warned him that his daughter had reached a watershed in her life. She was about to make far-reaching decisions and all he could do was pray for her happiness.

'Miss Rose, you know then?' Annie asked, as Rose burst into the kitchen. 'Madam is that happy now Mr Barney is home. There were so many new wounded they were short of beds.'

'Where is he?' Rose demanded, excitement sparkling in her eyes.

She had been planning to see him but that he was already here at Dower Cottage had to be a good omen.

'He's in the drawing-room with his mother but you can't go in with dirty boots,' Annie warned.

'I'm not stopping,' Rose called back. 'If you want to help, pack all of my things.'

Rose's rushed entry into the drawing-room had Mrs Tabley exclaiming in shock.

'What's the meaning of this? Have you completely forgotten the good manners I've been to so much trouble trying to drum into you?'

'Barney, I must talk to you,' Rose said, ignoring Mrs Tabley.

'Mother, leave us, please,' Barney ordered quietly.

Then as she began to fuss, he raised his voice, underlining his order by pointing to the door. Sobbing, calling for Annie who did not come, Mrs Tabley stumbled up the stairs to her room.

'Sit down, Rose,' he said firmly. Then seeing her hesitate he added sharply, 'Never mind the furniture! There are more important things than a bit of mud. Checking you were keeping your room tidy, Mother found this.'

Reaching into his pocket, he drew out the ribbon and his signet ring. He held them out towards her but ignoring them, she stared at him defiantly.

'It's over, Barney.'

Her tone was so matter-of-fact that he half smiled. Then his face hardened.

'So you're just like the two who let Jim and Andy down. I would never have thought you would have dumped me just because of my legs. I will eventually get their full use back, not that it seems you care.'

'It has nothing to do with your legs. If things had been different, I would have stuck by you, whatever state you were in.'

'What things?' he demanded harshly.

Looking down at her work-roughened hands, she spoke softly.

'It would never have worked, us marrying. We might have shared wonderful times together, but the war shattered all of that, made us both grow up. Even married to you, I would never be accepted by the circle you move in. They would look down on me.'

'I would never allow that to happen!'

'Then you, too, would be ostracised and

128

when all is said and done you, the manor, your mother, are all bound up too tightly with the past. You will want to continue things as they have always been and marrying a farmer's daughter would very definitely upset the apple cart!' she ended with a smile.

But Barney wasn't smiling.

'So my ring meant nothing to you.'

'I wore it because it was yours and you had sent it to me.'

'But you didn't wear it openly,' he accused, 'or all the time.'

Looking at him steadily, she did not realise her voice softened as she replied.

'There's a good reason for not wearing it now.'

'There's someone else, isn't there? Who is it? Dawson? I've seen the way he looks at you.'

She glanced away, not wanting him to even glimpse what she felt for Hugo. It was too private, too precious.

'It doesn't matter who he is, not now. He didn't come between you and me, for if we're honest, we were never really in love, were we? The war made us act impetuously as it did many people.'

Then before he could question further, she asked, 'And what about you? You and Sister Clark seem very friendly.'

'Don't change the subject!'

Standing up, she said firmly, 'As far as I'm concerned the subject of you and me is very firmly closed! Kate Clark would be much better at being Lady of the Manor than I would.'

As he shrugged, Rose heard Annie coming down the stairs.

'Goodbye, Barney. I'll always remember you with affection.'

He began to protest, but she had gone.

Slowly sliding the signet ring free of the ribbon, he replaced it on his little finger. Although he knew the past could not be recaptured, he mourned its passing. Rose had been such a great part of it, so much laughter, happiness. If only it could have continued. But then, a small voice reasoned, he never would have considered marrying her. What they had shared as they grew up could not have lasted into adulthood. The difference in their social positions would have become more and more apparent.

Although, out of duty to him, she had tried to learn the ways of the manor and his mother, if there had been no war, her independent spirit would never have agreed to such a thing. But his heart momentarily subdued his reasoning and he sighed. He envied the man she was going to. She would light his life joyously, something he doubted Kate Clark could do for him.

*   *   *

'Mother, I demand to know where Hugo is!'

Hampered by the bulk of her suitcase, Rose's stumbling run to the farm seemed to have taken for ever.

Having seen Hugo on the way to safety, Flora had sought the sanctuary of her distilling room. She needed to think, to be certain what to do for the best. Now she knew.

'Hugo will be in Worcester by now. I stopped a carrier and, glad of the money, he made room amongst his crates of chickens. You should have heard the commotion!'

'So he's gone then!'

Suddenly exhausted in both body and spirit, Rose collapsed on a chair.

'Rose, tell me, has this all been a bit of an adventure, perhaps to take your mind off Barney?'

'No! I never loved Barney. But I guess you realise that by now. I love Hugo and when this war is over, we'll be together, I know we will!'

'Why wait until then?' Flora asked quietly, taking both of Rose's hands.

'Rose, seize this moment. Make things work out for you instead of sitting back and just hoping. I told Hugo the name of the hotel in Worcester where I've stayed sometimes when your father and I have had words. I suggested he stay there tonight, before going to London tomorrow.'

Squeezing her mother's hand so hard that Flora cried out, Rose almost fell over her words.

'If I hurry, I'll be able to catch the last train!'

In actual fact, Hugo had never left the railway station, watching with increasing misery as every train came in, without the love of his life. As the last one of the day steamed in, he held his breath.

'Rose!'

His exultant shouts brought smiles from other passengers. Before she had stepped down on to the platform, he encircled her in his arms.

'You've come!' Then more seriously he added, 'Rose, I've got to know. In the cottage, you promised . . . It isn't like that time with Barney, is it?'

'No, my dearest love. This time, it most certainly is not a reluctant promise! We will be together, to face any hardship, and when this beastly war is over, we will have the rest of our lives, with each other.'